THE BLIND HEART

BOOKS BY STORM JAMESON

Novels

THE BLIND HEART

A MONTH SOON GOES

THE ROAD FROM THE MONUMENT

LAST SCORE

ONE ULYSSES TOO MANY

A CUP OF TEA FOR MR. THORGILL

THE HIDDEN RIVER

THE GREEN MAN

MOMENT OF TRUTH

BLACK LAUREL

BEFORE THE CROSSING

THE OTHER SIDE

CLOUDLESS MAY

THEN WE SHALL HEAR SINGING

COUSIN HONORE

THE FORT

EUROPE TO LET: THE MEMOIRS OF AN OBSCURE MAN

THE CAPTAIN'S WIFE

IN THE SECOND YEAR

LOVE IN WINTER

COMPANY PARADE

WOMEN AGAINST MEN

THAT WAS YESTERDAY

Other Books

THE WRITER'S SITUATION

THE JOURNAL OF MARY HERVEY RUSSELL

NO TIME LIKE THE PRESENT

Storm Jameson

THE
BLIND
HEART

HARPER & ROW, PUBLISHERS

NEW YORK AND EVANSTON

FIRST EDITION

LIBRARY OF CONGRESS CATALOG CARD NUMBER: 64-12686

B-O

THE BLIND HEART

1

In the whole wide promenade less than a dozen people were pretending that the March sun was stronger than the cruel north wind sharpening its razor on exposed skin, trying to strip the flesh from the bones, rattling the dry palm trees, fracturing the sea into glassy splinters falling like hailstones on the bare shingle. It blew from the Alps, invisible behind the circle of lower hills at the back of Nice, dry rocky slopes naked under their thin covering of snow.

The man walking rapidly along the side of the road nearer the sea either did not feel the wind or enjoyed it when it rasped his eyelids and dragged at the roots of his wide curled mustache. His face, with its jutting nose, and lines cut deeply into the heavy flesh, weather-darkened, was a masterpiece of good humor, the long mouth half-smiling, the eyes, deep-set under remarkably bossed lids, lively, with a yellowish gleam under the gray surface.

He passed a seated man, all of him except sponge-bag trousers and an arm in a black fleecy jacket hidden by the newspaper he was reading: the arm ended in a gloved hand which fumbled in the packet open beside him on the seat for sandwiches he appeared to swallow whole. Also beside him, on the ground, a small white dog watching, motionless, as sandwich after sandwich disappeared behind the copy of *Paris-presse*.

He walked on another fifty yards, turned, and came back: dog and man were still there, but the dog's spine had begun to sag under a weight of suspense.

"Hey, dog," he said loudly, "do you want to eat?"

Lowering his paper, the dog's master glared from a pair of eyes too small for the veined supercilious face, and gulped the last sandwich.

Laughing, a rich easy rolling sound, the other walked on.

He crossed the road, took a narrow side street and turned left into the rue de France. Here, in a house behind a dark courtyard, was the office of his lawyer, who was called Jouassaint. Here he was to meet that ruffian Larrau, Paul Larrau, and finish with him. All the old devil still had to do was write his name—if he could write—at the foot of the page, and he had been stalling for eight months, inventing new conditions, queries, delays, for the sheer joy of making a nuisance of himself.

But I foxed him, he thought, smiling: he never had the satisfaction of knowing what pleasure it would have given me to ring his withered neck.

In the windowless little room on the ground floor, Jouassaint's underclerk, young, plump, miraculously blonde, stood up. The light from the unshaded electric bulb over her head gave her yellow hair a greenish tinge, like tarnished metal.

"Good afternoon, Monsieur Michal."

"Good afternoon, Micheline." The glance he passed over her, from her hair to the shadowy cleft between breasts shaped like pears, small hard winter pears, thrust firmly up at the tip, was friendly and uncovetous. "Maître Jouassaint expects me."

"Yes, I know. Shall I take you up?"

"No need. I ought to know my way by now." He turned in the doorway. "Are they up there?"

"Monsieur Larrau and his lawyer? No. Not yet."

"The old sinner—let's hope he's not giving trouble."

Climbing the uncarpeted stairs, he controlled a spurt of rage. Don't get hot yet, he warned himself. The door of the lawyer's room was open. He walked in, and saw, or thought he saw, that nothing had gone seriously wrong. Jouassaint's gray face was not more discreetly that of an unfrocked priest than usual, and he was stroking his short beard, the texture and color of dry hay, as he did when he was satisfied.

"Larrau not here? Where is he?"

"It's all right, my dear sir, perfectly all right. They telephoned five minutes ago. He missed the bus he ought to have taken, and had only just reached the Rodiers' office, fuming and groaning. The elder Rodier will bring him along in twenty minutes or so—when he has had a rest."

"He doesn't need to rest," Michal said, grinning. "He has the energy of the devil he is."

"Well, sit down. Everything is ready. Brandy? A cigar?"

"Not before we're out of the wood."

"You're impatient."

"Oh. At my age the rope is getting short."

"If I didn't know you are sixty I should put you at forty-five or less. Larrau now, what's he?—he must be eighty."

"Seventy-nine. A goat, an old goat. Nothing is too much for him, he walks the four miles from his farm to the café every evening, and back, in all weathers, he drinks a single glass of red, the cheapest, and a black coffee. At home, he drinks only coffee, and that more barley than beans, with skim milk, and eats like a sparrow. Fifteen years ago he had *turns*—whatever they are—he was giddy, and he fell about the place, his sons thought he was going at last and licked their lips. But not he. Since then he's never had an hour's illness. He's reached the age when you don't die except by accident or a mistake. If you ask me, they'll all have one foot in the grave before he stumbles into his."

"He has how many sons?"

[3]

"Three. The two who live in the house, with their families, and the one who got away to Paris. That's when he—so they say—killed his wife. Oh, not on purpose. He locked her in an attic as a punishment and forgot to unlock it when he went off for five days, she daren't call out, the others thought she was with him, and by the time he got back she was past praying for. She'd given the boy money to go off—Larrau's money."

"I understand he has a quarter of a million in the bank."

"Not true. He never keeps money—he won't keep mine. He buys land, sheep—last year he bought Mazouillier's olive press. What use has he for money? He never buys clothes, grows what meat and wretched wine he needs, and he wouldn't give a farthing to a child. More land, more sheep, more anything you can grow up there. What he's worth, if he were sold up—ah, I don't know, nor, I'd say, does he. Or care."

Jouassaint did not answer. He sat digesting the information in his brain, greedier than his belly, which rarely made demands on him. Far from inhuman, he liked the man filling out the shabby leather armchair near him, and felt pleased that after eight months the deal with Paul Larrau was at last going through.

Larrau owned the small four-bedroom hotel in St.-Loup-de-Grâce where, over the years, Aristide Michal had worked up a restaurant to which people drove from Nice, Cannes, and much farther afield: it had deserved its one Michelin star, and had it been larger and more presentable it might have earned two. The old house itself had been a farmhouse, small, but it had traces of charm and dignity, and a Parisian businessman on holiday in the neighborhood had taken a fancy to turn it into a house for himself and his family to use during vacations. He had offered Larrau what the place was worth as a house, and then raised his offer to five million. Here he stuck.

It may only have been to tease Michal that the old fellow declared he was ready to sell, and asked him to match the offer if he did not want to be turned out. Possibly he had no

real intention of selling. But, step by step, between the prod-
dings of the Parisian's lawyer, and Michal's, he reached the
point of agreeing to let Michal buy the place. Again, possibly,
once he had made up his mind to sell he chose Michal only because he did not want to lose the café where he sat for four
hours every day over his single glass, playing belote with his—
absurd to call them his friends: he had none. Who the devil
knew what went on in that brain, dry and agile as a grasshopper,
torn between greed—the thought of turning the money into
land—and reluctance to oblige anyone whomsoever by doing
what he was asked?

He never in argument used the Parisian's name, but called
him "the foreigner."

In truth, not he but Michal was the foreigner. A Greek,
brought to France as a child—and naturalized in 1917 when he
was twenty-one under the name he now went by—his Greek
name, which appeared in one place in the documents under the
lawyer's supple thumb, had been Michalopoulos, Aristides
Michalopoulos, a name no odder than scores of Greek and Italian names scattered along this coast: they were less common
inland, in the savage country where St.-Loup-de-Grâce sheltered
its few houses and the Hotel Moderne Aristide on the south-
east-facing slope of a rocky hill.

Seeing Michal's long sun-blackened hand tapping the arm
of the chair, the lawyer smiled.

"Don't fret," he said gently. "Rodier assures me that there
can be no further hitch."

"I'll believe it when it comes off," Michal said.

He smiled, and stood up. Balancing his body lightly—that
well-nourished body, muscles covered by a thin layer of hard
flesh, skin gleaming as if polished—he walked as far as the
window and back. Jouassaint glanced at him with respect and
something near affection: the respect was for a body arrogant
even in its decline, a head of thick curled hair carried on a
powerful neck, a mouth as smooth as a young man's and white

strong teeth that made the lawyer's tongue touch regretfully
his own false set. The glance from Michal's yellowish-gray
eyes was direct and without a trace of servility or dour egoism.
Self-centered he might be, no doubt was—what sensible man
is not?—but with a rare joy in living.

It was the last that Jouassaint envied him.

"Shall you enlarge the place?" he asked.

"Not I! Eight tables is as many as I can do with, to cook
as it pleases me to cook." He laughed. "You'll go a long way to
find anything to beat my *poulet aux morilles,* or my *gratin de
langoustines Aristide.* Not even in Paris—don't talk to me about
Paris."

"You'd make your fortune there."

Michal gave him a brief half-contemptuous look, which said:
Don't try flattering me, it won't take.

"No. I'm a clever fellow in various ways, I work like a horse,
I prepare five let's say six dishes perfectly, I buy my coffee
green and roast it by handfuls for every order. But I know better
than to think I could run one of your places for rich foreigners,
where a Minister can take his most expensive bitch and feel
at home. That needs talents, an experience of the world, an
impudence, I don't possess—"

He broke off sharply. "I hear them."

He was right. A minute later the door was opened by Micheline, who flattened herself against it to avoid being crushed,
purposely or not, by the elderly Maître Rodier, his vast figure
bastioned in a corset which started under his armpits and went
as far as it conveniently could, smiling, his mouth stretched
above a gluttonous chin, his eyeballs pushed out by good living.
If he had been created to form a contrast with the ascetic Jouassaint, the creation was a ravishing success. None the less, the
two lawyers were of the same species: their understanding,
conveyed in a handclasp, a glance, was with each other, not
with either client.

The man he pushed in front of him, gently, a hand on one

[6]

sloping shoulder, was a quarter of his size, a scarecrow in a worn suit, with a scarf knotted round his threadbare neck in place of a tie. The skin of his face, crossed in every direction by dark cracks, like an old oven dish, was none the less fresh and rosy, his lips, drawn inward over toothless gums, were visible only as a brown line, and his fine predatory nose was as sharp as a knife. He had noticeably small and delicate hands and feet.

"Good afternoon, Monsieur Larrau," Jouassaint said, "how are you? Well, I can see for myself how you are. Fresh as the day. It's a pleasure to see you."

"Why shouldn't I look fresh?" Larrau said.

He had a laugh something between a scream and a hen's cackle; it pierced the eardrums. His own lawyer was well cushioned to endure it, but Jouassaint shuddered. He turned an imploring glance on Rodier.

"Can we get straight on with our formalities?" he murmured.

A tremor crossed the rich rolling stretch of the other's face, the movement of a worm under the soil. "There's just one point—"

Michal had been silent except for a single word of greeting addressed to Larrau. He bounded from his chair.

"You hear?" he shouted. "He's beginning again. Great God in heaven!"

"Wait," his lawyer said warningly, "wait until we know what it's about. Go on, please, maître."

Rodier passed a hand over his vast polished crane. "It's really nothing that need delay us. Or not for long. My client is prepared for everything, he is ready to sign all the necessary documents, he has only one minor condition he wishes to make, he—"

Unable to control himself, Michal struck the edge of the desk. "One condition! One more! And what is it this time? He wants me to lick his hands before I put the money in them, he wants it in gold, in platinum, he wants, he wants, he wants

[7]

double the money. He won't get it, I'm through with him, finished. Let him make a fool of someone else, I'm off."

Rodier's voice stopped him halfway across the room. "You're quite mistaken. We"—he sent his delighted client a cold glance —"have no idea of raising the price agreed. How could we? At this stage? All Monsieur Larrau asks is that the sum should be paid him in cash—not by check. It is unusual, but I see no overriding objection—we all have our fancies—and I trust we can agree, on this final point, with"—he paused briefly—"the same friendliness that has carried us this far in the negotiations. Maître Jouassaint?"

"I think I must talk this over with my client—"

"No," Michal interrupted. He had swallowed his rage. "I agree."

With pleasure, glancing sideways, he saw a look of bitter disappointment cross his tormentor's face. The old goat was hoping for a long argument, he reflected. Good!

He sat down again, crossing his hands on his knees, and let the two lawyers arrange between them that, tomorrow or the day after, the money would be available in this office, for Monsieur Larrau to see and handle it, since that was what he wanted; the papers would be signed at the same meeting, and the Hotel Moderne Aristide become—at last—his.

"I feel, Monsieur Larrau," said Rodier, "that you would like me to express your gratitude to Monsieur Michal for his willingness to gratify you."

"Not at all," Larrau said. He cocked his head on one side; a ray of sun striking over the top of the wicker blind glanced off his nose, which looked more lethal than ever. He went off into his screeching laugh. "I don't feel grateful. Why should I? If Monsieur Michal has agreed he did it to please himself, not me. I'm not obliged to thank him."

This amused Michal. "You're quite right," he said, and added, "Would you like me to give you a lift back to the village?"

"In your brute of a car? Not I. The bus is safer."

[8]

"As you please."

Jouassaint escorted his fellow lawyer and Larrau downstairs. He came back wiping his forehead on a large blue and white checked silk handkerchief. "My God, he's tough."

"Larrau? Oh. He's not a bad sort. Honest in his way. What he promises he does." He laughed. "He's not free with promises."

"Sit down a minute. I'll ring up the bank and talk to them —to the manager. They know all about it, but they don't know our friend Larrau. And five million francs is a certain amount of money."

"It's almost every penny I've saved," Michal said easily.

"You know—there was no need to use the whole sum. You could still, if you wish, borrow on it—"

"I know, I know. We've been into all that. I prefer to buy the place with what I have. I shall begin to save again—that's all. You know—it's a habit with me. I began at thirteen when I started as a waiter, and for the next dozen years I lived on scraps like a dog, without even knowing I was poor. It did me no harm. By then I had enough in my pocket to risk renting a hole-in-the-wall café in Marseilles. Then in 1929—I was thirty-three—I moved to St.-Loup and rented the place, it was nothing but the café then, from Larrau. Except for the war, for the ten months I spent chewing the skin off my knuckles in Evreux, I haven't moved since. Nor want to. The place suits me, it suits me to be deputy mayor—for the last five years—it suits me that the mayor, Favier, has his carrying business on his heart and leaves everything to me, I know what I'm doing, and I know what has to be done. Not a soul but trusts Aristide Michal to do the right thing for him. No, no, I'm happy, the life fits me like a glove, I have everything a reasonable man wants—I believe I'm reasonable—I have a bit of a temper, yes, but it's a flash and gone. You won't find *me* bearing grudges, or making my family wet their trousers when I raise my voice. Never."

Your family, the lawyer thought, amused. He knew that Michal's wife was not his wife, nor the young fellow he called "my son" his son. Listening with pleasure to the full deep voice, he thought: He boasts, but he knows himself.

"How is your boy?" he asked politely. "Let's see—he's what age now?"

"Nineteen. Going on twenty. Sixteen years this coming June since I found him, asleep and still crying, on the side of the road ten miles south of Châteauroux. Whether he'd been left there on purpose, whether his people had lost him—they'd been choking that road, the poor sinners, on foot and in every sort of car and cart, for three days, and there'd been some bombing— heaven alone knows. No one will ever know."

Thank God, he added silently, feeling in his mouth the sour taste of the anxiety with which, for years, until it began to seem the most improbable of nightmares, he expected someone to turn up, an uncle, a mother, demanding the boy.

He had been speaking in the voice a young man might have used to describe a woman, moved and diffident.

With something like envy—envy and derision—the lawyer thought: About that boy he's not sane. It's a joke.

He got up and went into the next room to telephone to the bank.

2

For twelve miles after he left Nice, he drove rapidly along the spoiled coast, paying no attention to it except to raise his hand to a man he had known and despised for years, the Italian proprietor of a shoddy one-night hotel, who saluted him from a doorway. He was turning over in his mind—without repenting —a folly he had just allowed himself.

Shortly after it had crossed the stony bed of the Var, his road turned inland and began to climb toward Vence. He swayed past a bus, forcing it to drive with a wheel over the ditch; he caught a glimpse of Larrau's gargoyle of a head turned to the window, and recovered his good temper. After Vence, he was driving on a very different sort of road, steeper, narrow, with every few hundred yards an acute-angled turn between a precipice and a dry hillside fanged with gray lichened rocks. In summer, the light striking down on these rocks and calcined slopes sent out ripples of heat to break down and deform the outlines of the distant higher hills and the few pines and dry straggling herbs, and scorch the rocks so that the lichen rubbed off them like singed hair. Now, in March, the air, cleared by the north wind, pinned to the ground every frost-riven stone, every tall ghost of a plant, every tree trunk, entirely naked. At one turn or the next, the lower hills drew apart for a minute to allow a dazzlingly white crest to be seen piercing a sky which by contrast became as suave as a pigeon's throat.

He could have taken the longer and better road, but he was impatient.

At the height of three thousand feet the land flattened into a long narrow plain of short grass: except that it turned and twisted on itself as if it had acquired a habit it could not shake off, the road stretched across it for five or six miles: then, in front and on the right, another corroded snow-spattered peak, split by a deep gorge.

Where the road to St.-Loup-de-Grâce turned sharply left, with the stream below it at the bottom of the narrow gorge, a single stone bore two names, the brothers Jean and Firmin Truchi, "ici fusillés, victimes de la barbarie Nazi," and a single line like a cry: SOUVIENS-TOI: below it, a withered handful of narcissus.

Exactly at this point a cart track, rutted and full of stones, came in from the pasture to the left, part of Larrau's land, and he saw a figure stumbling along it, a woman in a dark cloak. He recognized it, and stopped the car to wait for her.

"Ah, Madeleine, you're just in time. Get in."

"Thank you, Monsieur Michal, thank you."

Sitting beside him, she leaned against the door as if to leave as wide a space as possible between herself and him. It was her immediate response to any gesture: a too-sudden movement toward her made her start back and begin to lift an arm to protect herself. She had brought the habit with her from the prison camp in East Prussia, and eleven years was not long enough to cure it. It was perhaps incurable.

Also incurable was the attitude to her of the villagers who had known her as child and girl, until in 1938 she married the young clerk on holiday from Paris and went away with him. When, in 1945, she was set down in the village by the driver of the van from the Receiving Center in Nice, and they were expected to welcome a skeleton in ragged shirt and trousers picked up somewhere on the way, hair hanging in wisps round a vacant face, the wrinkled flesh of her body covered with suppurating ulcers, scarcely one man or woman had been able to endure looking at her. Both her parents had died during her absence, she had no other relatives. The doctor took her into his house. His wife confessed to horror at the spectacle of this leprous object lying between her linen sheets, but behaved well enough, and slowly, slowly, Madeleine Clozel built a frail bridge between the prison camp and a life which might, but for one circumstance, have become ordinary, even normal.

That circumstance was the child she had seen for a few hours, at its birth, and not since.

It is hard, at the best of times, for people to forgive anyone who reminds them that unbearable cruelty, unbearable suffering, are as much a fact of life as joy. What the inhabitants of St.-Loup-de-Grâce could not forgive her was their original horror of the victim. They felt about her very much as they would have felt if the two young Truchis, pushing the stone off them with fleshless fingers, had returned. They accepted her, yes; a few were even kind: in time it seemed that she was again part of the village. But the distance, the hesitation, the impulse of recoil, still hung, a shadow, behind the eyes of most of the men and women who watched her going about her work, wrapped, even in summer, in her cloak, as though she were always cold, a woman in the middle thirties who might, with a skin as colorless and ravaged as hers, have been any age.

Nothing to be done about it. The victim is always in the wrong—because always a reproach. To the human kind itself.

Aristide Michal was one of the very few who did not feel the reproach. Perhaps because the gaiety, the ease, the deep

[13]

warmth, in which his own ironic tenacity had its root was strong enough to embrace even cruelty. He had done more for Madeleine Clozel than anyone except Dr. Bertin himself, by giving her, when she was barely fit to work, the job of mending the hotel linen, arguing—and he was right—that what she needed most was a link with everyday life.

She earned her living now as a sewing woman and dressmaker, a poor living but enough.

Driving, more slowly now, as the road worsened, becoming narrower and crazily uneven, he asked her,

"When do you go to Germany? Tomorrow, isn't it?"

"Yes."

"My poor Madeleine, it is an ordeal for you."

"Monsieur Vincent will be with me."

He hesitated. To talk to her of hope, now, was perhaps the wrong thing. After a moment he said,

"You have been very patient."

She smiled—her smile was the only thing she had carried over from her old life. "And what else could I have been?"

The village lay on two levels, the upper level a large square of beaten earth, mud to the hocks in a wet month, in summer an acre of dust: here were the ugly church with its tenth-century crypt and in the porch a few fragments of stone with the all but obliterated remains of an inscription in Greek, the one-story mairie, the Cooperative, and the school. From here the road dropped to a lower level, descending steeply between the oldest houses, a few empty, all of them iron-gray, shabby, indestructible, and straightened out at last into the street—more lane than street—that ended in Michal's hotel. Madeleine Clozel lived in the steepest part, on the way down: her house, one of the smallest and oldest in the village, had only two rooms, one above the other, with a kitchen and a shed of sorts at the back. The front door opened into the lower room, and the stairs to the upper started from a corner of the kitchen, turning round and inside the three-foot wall of the chimney.

He set her down at her door.

"Good luck for Thursday."

"Thank you."

As he jolted, swaying, along the lower street, heads were thrust from windows and the doors of the three dark little shops: a woman fingering a bolt of cloth in the draper's turned from it to call at the top of her voice,

"Has he signed?"

The wife of the mayor, she was the only person in the village impudent enough to ask outright what everybody was dying to know. Smiling, showing all his strong teeth, Michal made a gesture that might have meant anything, but to the leery hard-grained inhabitants of St.-Loup said: Not yet.

A man who had jumped on to the doorstep of a house to get out of the way of the car—another Truchi, second cousin to the victims of etc etc, who was the village policeman, also the plumber and roofer—spat in the gutter as a mark of exasperation and sympathy.

Where the street came to a stop in front of the hotel, it widened to form a small irregularly shaped square, cobble-stoned. In fine weather Michal set tables here: a rough stone wall ran round two sides of it, making a parapet which over-hung the least steep part of the hill, scored immediately below the village by a few rows of derelict terraces where less than a score of useless olive trees survived: below them the hill fell steeply down, far down, flowing into the folds of other hills, coiling and uncoiling into the valley toward a thin glittering line of sea like the upturned edge of a knife.

As always when he came back to it, Michal stood here a moment, looking at the small hotel with the affection of a husband for the wife he is used to and trusts. Now that the place was so nearly his, a hard swell of excitement sprang in the pit of his stomach. Trying to calm himself, he thought: A coat of limewash on the end wall, and in April get Truchi on to the lower roof.

The lowest of the three stories was built into the side of the hill, below the level of the street, with iron stanchions support-ing a jutting bay. Here were kitchen, storerooms, and larder, and the room he had made into a restaurant, its new window looking down over the broken lines, planes, curves, shadows, of the fantastically beautiful and worn-out landscape, furrowed by age, quivering in the light or black and frozen in the darkness.

Here, too, next to the restaurant, was his son's room, little wider than a passage, but with the same view.

On the street level was the café, with its square marble tables, sawdust on the floor, the great iron stove, the bar counter: at the side farthest from the little square, his own bedroom. Above were the four small bare rooms occupied in spring and summer by tourists willing to do without a bath, and sometimes by diners who preferred to sleep off their meal here rather than drive home, bellies overfull and heads ringing.

Before he came here the place was a drinking pub, the Café de la Bastide. He kept the name for a year, then renamed it: Auberge de la Bastide. Then, after three years, when he started the restaurant, it became the Hotel Moderne Aristide—his name, his creation, crowned, five years ago, in 1951, by its single star.

At this moment he felt that not one of the more than forty years of straining sinews and soul since he began his working life had been less than happy, rising now to a secret intoxica-tion, a ferocious sensual ecstasy.

Out of half-superstitious prudence, he tried to reduce it to order before going in: it retreated to the back of his eyes where the yellow glint fanned out into a small leaping flame.

Lifting from the back of the car the big leather portmanteau lent him by a protesting Jouassaint, he carried it directly through the café to his bedroom.

Its two compartments were filled to the edges by bundles of notes. He was still transferring these to the heavy old-fashioned safe he kept in a curtained recess behind the bed when his wife came into the room: he showed her what he was doing, and told her all that had happened at the lawyer's and since.

Sitting down on the side of their bed, she smoothed her hair back, looking at herself in the glass over the chest of drawers, and beginning to laugh. The gleam of her teeth, eyes, and wide firm lips was that of a young woman.

"Why on earth did you bring it here? Why didn't you leave it where it was or with that Jouassaint? You must be off your head to drag so much money about the country."

Her voice had been the first thing about her to seduce him. It reached him from the darkness of an alley between two houses in a poor street behind the Cannebière; he was walking back to his room at three in the morning, in no mood to be seduced, tired out and all but asleep on his feet. Shocked awake, he stood still.

Even now, after so many years, at certain moments, using certain words, it affected him like a finger stroking his spine.

He looked at her, smiling, almost shamefaced. "Well, if you want to know, I had a fancy to handle it myself before giving it to the old goat."

It's mine, he thought, it's my whole life to this moment. He weighed one of the bundles on his palm. My fortunate life.

"Is it all there?" she asked. "The lot?"

"Yes. I'm paying it over tomorrow afternoon—unless Larrau decides to die tonight."

"Him? He's never going to die."

He fitted in the last bundle, locked the safe and put the key back on the ring he carried in his inner pocket. Getting up from his knees, he stood close to her beside the bed. He guessed that she had come from the kitchen: warm, her body gave off a curiously delicate smell, a little like cedar, a smell younger than she was. Like many women in this part of Provence, she had the profile of a Roman matron, the thick column of neck, straight stubborn nose, pure rather low forehead: seen from the front, the lower part of her face was not in the least classical—

[17]

a boyish chin and a long mouth, surprisingly long: two deep lines ran from its corners to her nostrils. At fifty-five they were the only noticeable lines on her face, and gave it a slightly sardonic expression, as though she were mocking her age and the fullness of her body below the still narrow waist.

When Michal picked her up in Marseilles, she was twenty-five, ill, half-starved, nothing but gray skin and bone, the wife of a hotel waiter who had left her and gone off to the States with an American woman staying in the hotel. She had tried to get work and failed, she was ill, and her first efforts at selling herself were also a failure. Perhaps, at first, she felt for Michal only the gratitude of a deserted starving animal to the man who gives it food and a home. But very soon, as her health and energy returned, they shared a passion for each other's bodies, warm and brutal, which only very slowly ripened into the affection of use and kindness.

For all they knew, her husband was still alive. They had never tried to find out. Neither thought of their relationship as less than lifelong. What changes endures.

For a time, Michal hoped for a family, at least a son. Some idiosyncrasy in Lotte's strong body produced only miscarriages, and after four of these there was no more hope.

She was thirty-nine—with the face and body of a young woman—when Michal brought her the four-year-old boy he had picked up on a road down which, for three days, the clotted stream of refugees and demoralized soldiers had been moving like one of those floods that lay waste a countryside.

Why had he brought him all the way to St.-Loup instead of handing him in at the nearest police station? For the simplest reason in the world. Because, when he picked up the child, sleeping, and crying in its sleep, it had opened one hand and closed it round Michal's finger, and ceased to cry. It was only later that he noticed its sex and what it looked like.

The child was as beautiful as a Greek statue: even Paul

Larrau, seeing him one day when he came to the café, was struck speechless, and recovered his tongue to say only,

"You'd better look out. It can't last."

Either he was backward for his four years, or shock had disordered his memory; all he could tell them was his age and Christian name, Max, and that he lived with "mummie and nunkie," in "our house." Not even the name of the town or village. One of his torn garments had the label of a Belgian manufacturer of cheap clothes, and that was as much and as little evidence as they had about him.

After a time they began to talk of him as "our child," and settled on the day he was picked up as his fourth birthday. They renamed him—Philippe.

Possibly Michal loved him more than he would have loved a child of his flesh, since nothing, no irritating resemblance, no sexual jealousy, clouded his pride in a creature given them, as the priest said, by God Himself.

"Where is Philippe?" he asked.

"Philippe?" Her voice prolonged the word into a caress. "He went off half an hour ago on his Vespa, to Grasse. He'll be home round about ten."

"That Vespa," Michal grumbled, smiling.

The boy had two passions, for speed and dancing. Using his Vespa as if it were winged, he went everywhere, Grasse, Cannes, Nice, even Marseilles, to dance—in summer leaving the hotel at eleven at night to return in time for breakfast, still lively, all smiles and light talk.

"He prepared the vegetables."

"Oh, that," Michal said.

One of the eight tables in the dining room was occupied every evening by the same guest, an Englishman living, alone with a manservant, in a house less than a mile from the village. The servant, a middle-aged Arab the Englishman brought with him from Tunis, where he had been living before he came to

St.-Loup in 1945, was either unbelievably reserved or stupid, no one had ever heard him use a sentence longer than five or six words. In shops he pointed to what he wanted, and paid from a small canvas money bag he wore tied round his waist under his shirt. He haggled, too, and never—though invariably defeated—gave up the habit. Yet no one doubted that the Englishman was well off. To begin with, an elderly idle Englishman must be rich, and, secondly, his car was large and immensely luxurious. In the evening when it fetched him from his house, it had to be left in the upper square, from where the Arab supported, half-carried, him to the hotel.

His name—George Leighton—was unknown to Jouassaint, who prided himself on knowing the income, profession, and past of every Englishman living within fifty miles of Nice. He was old rather than elderly, as old as Larrau, and a great deal frailer, emaciated, his neck a bundle of cords, his face grooved deeply from the temples to the thick arched nose, and from the high cheekbones to the root of the nostrils. A long mouth, drawn far down at the ends, cut the lower half of the face like another groove in the paper-thin layer of yellow flesh. The whole face, in repose—if repose is only another word for absence of change—was a mask of refusal, enmity, suspicion, wariness. In profile, he was an odd mixture of bird of prey and camel.

A cruel face, Lotte insisted. This Michal doubted, although he had heard cruel remarks drop from that lipless mouth.

One evening, when a handsome elegant Frenchwoman at one of the tables had been talking in a clear carrying voice about a politician with whom she seemed to be more than friendly, Leighton said afterwards,

"I know the type. She has had her womb cut out by a venal surgeon to be able to enjoy herself, and she enjoys nothing and no one, she works in other people, in a man, like a gangrene, like pus."

Little as Michal knew about him, he knew more than anyone except, possibly, the Arab servant. He knew, for instance, that

Leighton was a writer—or that, at any rate, he was writing one book, very slowly, apparently with the greatest difficulty or reluctance, since for months at a time he did not touch it.

This evening when he sat down and unfolded his napkin, he looked up at Michal and said indifferently,

"A good day. None of your Bellet, I'll have a bottle of the Corton."

"Ah, it's gone well today, the book?"

"Very well indeed."

"Good."

What the devil, he wondered, can the old fellow be writing? The story of his life? But has he had a life?

He brought the wine and allowed himself to accept the glass offered him. On another evening he would politely have refused. He disliked gifts to which he could make no return, and on the one occasion when, going to see the Englishman who was in bed with a fever, he had taken with him a bottle of decent claret, he read in the other's constrained smile only suspicion and annoyance.

"I, too, have had a good day," he said.

"Oh. He's signed!"

"No. But for tomorrow it's certain."

"Can you be certain of anything with him?"

"Ah, yes. This afternoon he caught a smell of the money. He'll sign."

"He's taken his time."

Michal smiled. "When you believe, as he does, that you still have a lifetime left, you can afford to annoy other people by dawdling."

"If I believed that—" Leighton began. He stopped, and went on in a simple voice, without a trace of irony, "My friend, I think about dying as I thought about the journey here when for a number of reasons it became time to leave Tunis—it's a bore and has to be done, but it's final, you won't have the trouble of doing it again."

Is he telling the truth? Michal wondered lightly. Yes. He doesn't need to boast.

Three other tables were now occupied. He went back to the kitchen, and sent Lotte upstairs to serve. The boy, Truchi's son, he had taken into the hotel, was as yet too clumsy. Philippe, if he had been here, would have stayed in the kitchen: he was a hard worker, no man ever had a better son, but he disliked waiting on people, and Michal did not press him.

Leighton rarely went home immediately after dinner. On most evenings when he left the dining room he sat down in the café upstairs to drink and play belote or bezique with Monsieur Pibourdin, the manager of the Cooperative, the doctor, Félix Bertin, and Monsieur Vincent. Blaise Vincent was the schoolmaster, as well as the secretary of the mairie, and the doctor's closest friend; born on the same day, brought up next door to one another, sent to the same schools, they had married sisters —it was said: tossing for the prettier of the two—were both now middle-aged respected widowers, and when they were together made no effort to remember their age and state.

The cardplayers sat round a table twice the size of any other in the room: in May it was dragged to the far end, into the window, and stayed there until the end of November, when it was moved back to its present place between the iron stove and the bar. Larrau, who despised bezique and only played belote, sat with them, spinning out his glass of rough red wine and cup of black coffee, until midnight. They tolerated him— Leighton, indeed, liked him, or pretended to.

Toward half past nine tonight Michal came upstairs and sent home the barmaid known to them all only as "old nanny goat," a creature she resembled closely enough—both in looks and in the powerful smell given off by her every movement—to have been alarming if she were not so stupid and amiable. He never took a hand in the game, and in the café drank as little as Larrau himself, but he was one of the circle to such a point that

[22]

on the rare occasions when he could not be present it broke up at the melancholy and unchristian hour of ten or eleven.

"Here he comes," said Pibourdin.

He watched with an involuntary envy the ease with which Michal moved a heavy bench that had been pushed out of its place, lifting it with one hand and setting it down again noiselessly.

"My God, I wish I had your strength," he said.

"Well, why haven't you?"

"My heart—"

"Nothing wrong with your heart, my dear fellow," the doctor interrupted, smiling. "You coddle yourself."

As he came into the café Michal had seen that one of the cardplaying circle was not there—the schoolmaster. He was on the point of asking why when Larrau went off into his screech of laughter.

"Our friend Michal is as strong as an ox," he said, "and cunning—you ought to hear how he beat me down to the last farthing. I'd be a ruined man if he was the only creature I did business with."

"If ever," said Michal, "I meet the man able to cheat you, I'll run for my life."

There's something both crafty and simple about him when he's happy, the doctor thought. He watched Michal curl round his finger the ends of his thick mustache, smiling yellowish eyes half-closed over the gleam of excitement and satisfaction. This was how he looked during an election—his only other passion, and a bare second to his pleasure in his hotel, was for politics, on which he spent as much shrewdness as would have made a millionaire of him if he had been one quarter as interested in money as he was in managing the local electors for their own good.

All the members of the little circle—except the Englishman —were members of the village council. And all, except the absent Vincent, were content to be under his thumb.

"Where," asked Michal, "is Vincent? Hasn't he been here this evening?"

"He's ill," the doctor said shortly. "A dose of flu. I went to look at him again on my way here. He'll be in bed two or three days. With his one lung he can't take risks."

"Then who is going with Madame Clozel to Frankfurt tomorrow?"

There was a silence—uneasy. Not that any of them, except possibly the doctor, felt any personal responsibility for Madeleine Clozel. The uneasiness was nothing more than an unlocalized feeling of discomfort, starting up whenever they were forced to recall the bare story of her life since the day in August, 1943, when she and her husband were arrested in Paris by the Germans, who mistook him for a far more important figure in the Resistance; he died in a few days of the attention they paid him, and she was deported—to East Prussia, to become a laborer on a farm. Here, in March, with unspeakable difficulty, she gave birth to her child, in the cold windowless outhouse. Moved by some impulse—pity? discomfort?—the German woman took it from her into the house. She even asked the mother, who seemed to be dying, whether she had a name for the child. "Jean," the young woman breathed. The other woman nodded. After a week the farmer asked the authorities to relieve him of a worker too sick to be any use, and she was sent to the camp near Ravensbrück, from which place she returned as the village tried not to remember her, fleshless, repulsive, so little like a human being that she roused, even in the gentle, more disgust than pity. That, too, it preferred not to remember.

Expelled from their farm in 1945, the German couple disappeared. It had taken more than nine years of search by the French Red Cross and the international refugee organization to find them, resettled in a village near Frankfurt. They had the boy.

His mother's first hours of trembling incredulous joy were also the last she was allowed. When the refugee organization petitioned an American High Commission court in Munich to return her child to her, it refused. Stupefied by the decision, she could not believe this either. But, five months later, the Court of Appeals at Frankfurt handed down the same refusal. Two out of the three judges were against her. Neither court had wanted to hear her.

"Why," people in the village asked her, half surprised, half sarcastic, "didn't you go there all the same, and scream, and insist on being heard? You haven't even seen your son!"

"I didn't think—" she began, and stopped, staring at them with eyes as vacant as those they had found so unnerving and disagreeable when she came back—seeming vacant, because what moved behind them at that time bore no likeness to anything they had imagined. And indeed there were moments when she felt more afraid of the world she had returned to than she had felt in the concentration camp, and more alone. It was not only her memories that divided her from these men and women who knew her when she was a child: the real barrier was the absence of a common language. Words to tell them why she had been afraid to go did not exist—in any language.

"I hadn't the money to travel all that way," she said at last.

But now the same three judges had decided to hear what she had to say. This, the third—and final—hearing, was her first chance to assert herself and her rights. Assert herself? Open the door of its cage for a captive animal to rush out and more likely than not it will recoil, in fear. The official who came from Nice to see her and make the arrangements to send her to Frankfurt said, when he got back to his office:

"They'll never give her the boy. She's not right in the head."

He had said it, too, to Dr. Bertin, who made no comment. Remembering it again now, the doctor wondered what would become of her if, on Thursday, she had to realize that she had lost her one and only throw.

"In my opinion, they should leave the boy where he is," Pibourdin said. "A boy of twelve, a young Boche—what else is he by now?—it's nothing short of insane to bring him away. He hasn't a devil's chance in hell of doing any good here. If Madame Clozel had asked my opinion I'd have given it to her."

The tone in which he spoke was intended to distract them from recalling that during the Occupation he had been less ill-disposed to these Boches. It had, naturally, the opposite effect.

"Opinions are among the few things you enjoy giving," Bertin said.

"And you're wrong," Michal said quietly, "she's his mother, she has a right to him. Nothing in the world, nothing, nothing, counts so much as a family. Talk to me about nations and all that! Bladders of air! Only families mean something—humanly speaking."

The glance Leighton gave him would have chilled a furnace. In an arrogantly well-bred voice, one he rarely used, he said,

"Rubbish. Absurd rubbish. More lies, more cruelty, more hatred, go on inside families than anywhere else. I detest all mysticism. Mysticism about the family more than any other."

Michal smiled.

"Personally," said Larrau, "I wouldn't cross the street to find a child. There are too many children, far too many, and most of them will grow up rascals, liars and hypocrites. What does it matter whether one of them lives his unnecessary life here or in some other country?"

As if speaking to himself, the doctor said:

"Possibly we owe a certain debt to Madeleine Clozel and her husband. He may not have done a great deal, but he died heroically."

"Nonsense," Larrau said dryly. "I don't owe him anything at all. Did I ask him to resist and get himself killed? He had only to hold his tongue and go on minding his own business. But he wanted to cock snooks at the Germans—or why did he do it? Well, let him. But I don't respect him for it. Not I!"

Pibourdin looked at him with smiling malice. "You don't like heroes?"

"I don't like being expected to pay them for something I never wanted them to do for me!"

Frowning, Michal said,

"A fine country it would be if every man in it thought as you do."

"Not at all! It would be peaceful. I don't interfere with anyone. Why should I? People don't interest me. I've had to rely on myself all my life, I had no one else. If two idiots start a quarrel, what has it to do with me? No, no, I don't like heroes. They get too many other people into trouble."

"He's right," Leighton said calmly. "I never do things for other people. Never. Let them get out of their troubles as they got into them—by their own efforts. Why should I trouble myself? At my age."

"Yet you gave yourself considerable trouble to help Madame Clozel," the doctor said slyly. "You wrote her letters for her to the Red Cross and the refugee people, you drove into Nice a dozen times to talk to them, and you encouraged her to appeal again. What's more, you paid Blaise Vincent's expenses to go to both hearings."

"Oh, that!" Leighton said. "Are we playing this game, or aren't we?"

"Let's get on with it," Larrau said, grinning.

"One thing about this business alarms me," the doctor said. "After the second hearing Blaise told me something he hasn't dared to tell Madame Clozel. It seems that what swung two of the judges to decide against her was the boy's own despair and rage at the mere thought of leaving his, what d'y'call them, foster parents. Apparently they treated him as their son and brought him up well and carefully, he's happy—the last thing he wants is to be handed back to a mother he doesn't know from Adam and Eve. Until this caught up with them he didn't know the German pair weren't his mother and father."

"What did I tell you?" Larrau said. He laughed.

"Are they the same judges?" asked Leighton.

"As the last time? Yes."

"Poor woman."

"Are we going on playing?" said Larrau.

[27]

"Right, right. Go on, we'll go on."

"Not I," Pibourdin said. "I must go, I have to get up at six to drive into Marseilles, to persuade half a dozen fools that I know my business better than they do."

He did not leave at once. After a minute or two, when Michal was behind the bar, he got up from his chair and, leaning on the counter, began to talk in his soft voice, smiling innocently, as he did when he had a maliciously amusing story on his tongue.

"That boy of yours makes friends very easily, doesn't he?"

Michal looked at him. "Why not? He's friendly and good-tempered."

"Two evenings ago when I was in Nice I saw him coming out of the Casino with two men, one an Algerian, and a couple of women. The men—well, I'd say that they didn't need to earn a living, they let the women do that for them, as magnificent a couple of skinners as I have ever seen, dressed for the job, and neither one of them over twenty-five. One of them had large eyes like a mare."

"Well?"

Disconcerted by the tone, Pibourdin said amiably,

"Philippe appeared to be on the best of terms with them—the mare especially. He's a nice boy. If I were you I'd drop him a word. Good night."

"Good night."

Watching Pibourdin go, moving his large soft body with the prudence of a hypochondriac, Michal shrugged off his moment of fury. No spiteful old woman was as malicious and untrustworthy as Pibourdin, he exuded scandal as helplessly as he sweated and panted on a warm day. Usually there was a grain of fact in his inventions, but by no means always. I'll speak to the boy, he thought easily.

To cool himself, he went outside. The wind had dropped, but it was bitterly cold, under a black sky, fractured by stars. For a moment he thought that the figure he saw vaguely, moving at the end of the dark street, was Pibourdin. Then he realized that it was coming toward the hotel, a cloaked figure, half running. Madeleine Clozel. She reached him, breathless.

"Come inside," he said, "come and get warm."

"No." She laid a hand on his arm—she who hated to touch or be touched. "What luck! I didn't want to come into the café. Did you know that Monsieur Vincent is ill, in bed?"

"The doctor told us so just now."

Her eyes did not move from his face. "He was going to Frankfurt with me."

"I know." To be there with you when they explain that the boy doesn't want to have anything to do with you.

Her hand tightened its grip. "How can I go alone!"

"The defense lawyer is there already, isn't he?"

"Yes. I don't know him."

"It's a long journey, but quite simple, you know. And you'll be looked after when you get there."

"Monsieur Michal—"

She stopped. He knew why she had come, what she wanted of him, and the thought made him savagely impatient. It's too much, he said to himself.

"Would you like me to come with you?"

"Oh," she said under her breath, "if you would!"

He sighed. "Very well."

"There's no one else I could ask. And, you know, I am a coward . . ."

He knew a great deal more than was comfortable. You are a fool to involve yourself, he thought, vexed. What the old goat says about you when he hears will be less scurrilous than you deserve. And what Blaise Vincent chooses to do in his business, no need for you to throw yourself into his place because you haven't the nerve to tell the woman she can perfectly easily go alone. . . . Briefly he wondered what terrified her the more, the idea of seeing her child or the idea of hearing German voices again. He said gently,

"You have as much courage as you need, my dear Madeleine."

He had noticed, before this, that, to survive grief or punishment, many seemingly fragile women are able to call on a patience, a nervous energy, a disconcerting insistence on living, even a kind of stupidity, which makes them hard to kill. Few women die of grief.

He questioned her about the arrangements Vincent had made with her, and when, almost without thanking him, she had gone, swallowed up in a few seconds by the darkness, he went back into the café, he decided to say nothing to Larrau and the others. Lotte could tell them, and telephone to Jouassaint, when he had left.

It was close on midnight and he was alone in the café when he heard Philippe's Vespa in the empty street. He waited, listening, when it jerked to a stop, to the noise of the shed door being opened and closed, and the young man's light rapid steps crossing the road to the hotel.

Philippe came in, smiling. He asked instantly,

"Has he signed?"

"No. But he will tomorrow. That is to say—" He broke off, and said, "You were going to be back at ten."

"I'm sorry. Did you need me?"

"No."

He watched as the young man moved swiftly about the room, collecting glasses from the tables and piling them on the counter. His color heightened by the rush through the cold air, the fine down of his skin, on his cheeks and between his eyebrows, was noticeable. Even when you live with it, there is no getting used to so much beauty. Larrau's tart hope had been disappointed; the flawlessly beautiful child had become the handsome youth, with features of extreme delicacy and strength, with fair hair brushed back from the rounded forehead and small ears, and a short fair mustache drawing attention to the beauty of mouth and nose. But it was not only perfection of modeling; there was some trace of feeling, in the eyes, on the lips, which gave the whole face a sensuous caressing charm, hard to define in words which have to do duty for so many ordinary well-composed good looks.

He is out of place here, Michal thought abruptly. But where wouldn't he be?

"Go to bed, dad. I'll clear up."

"What kept you?"

"I told Ti I was going into Grasse, but I changed my mind when I got there and went to Nice. Does it matter?"

He had never called Lotte anything but Ti, his first childish name for her. For some reason this pleased her, but had once vaguely disappointed Michal, whose feeling for the family was almost religious. He had no other religion.

"That reminds me," he said. "Monsieur Pibourdin has a story of seeing you two evenings ago in Nice with four types—Algerians and their women. Outside the Casino. Who were they?"

Philippe opened his eyes widely, and laughed, the clearest frankest sound in the world.

"He's a liar. They weren't Algerians and I wasn't in the Casino. We'd been next door, having a cassis. One of the chaps was Doucier, you remember him, dad, he came here one year with his family, from Bordeaux, the others were friends of his from, oh, I forget where, and one of the women was quite old, forty if she was a day. I ran into them in the street."

"Trust friend Pibourdin," Michal said. He laughed.

They heard Lotte's steps on the flight of stone stairs to the lower floor. She came into the room, pushing back with a finger the thick black curl falling out of its comb, yawning, a yawn which widened into a smile when she saw Philippe. Just as she reached them, her foot caught in a chair, and she stumbled and fell. Stooping, he straddled her body and picked her up, heavy as she was, as easily as if she were a child. She laughed, and put both arms round his neck, letting him lift her to her feet.

"Why are you so late?"

"Never mind that," Michal said. "Listen, you two, I'm going off early tomorrow—taking Madeleine Clozel to Frankfurt . . ."

He explained himself, very briefly, too impatient to go into the question why he had let himself in for this tiresome affair—in fact, embarrassed, knowing too well the figure of a fool he was going to cut with every sensible man and woman in the village—and told his wife what to do. To telephone to the lawyer, and either go herself or send Philippe to talk to old Larrau.

"He'll bray like a donkey, and enjoy himself so much, telling you what an ass I am, that he'll be in a good temper for a week."

"When will you get back?" asked Philippe.

"Let's see. We'll be in Frankfurt Wednesday afternoon. The hearing is for Thursday. If they give the boy to her—which is far from certain—he'll need a few hours, I suppose, before they hand him over. We'd start back on Saturday and reach Cannes Sunday night again. I'll wire you on Thursday—after the hearing."

"At the worst," Philippe said, "I mean the worst for Madame Clozel, you'll get back Saturday night. Otherwise Sunday."

"That's right."

"Well, go and get some sleep. You'll need it."

Stroking the boy's face with one finger, Lotte said gently, "And you, too, my dear. Go to bed."

In their bedroom, she packed a change of clothes for Michal, then undressed and sat down before the glass to brush her hair and smooth a little cream over her face and throat. Sitting upright, head thrown back, her body, above the waist and springing thighs, still slender, she stirred in him something between admiration and gratitude. So much warmth and kindness in a ripe body, so much frank unhurried pleasure. He began to pull off his own clothes.

His hand came on the ring of keys.

"Here," he said, "I won't take these with me to Frankfurt.

[32]

Put them in one of your drawers. Don't carry them round with you."

"Ah, yes—they'll be safer left here."

Later, in the darkness, when he passed his hands over this arrogantly healthy body, well-nourished, smooth, he thought for less than an instant of its wretchedness when he first knew it.

"You're happy, aren't you?" he said—not quite knowing why he had said it.

There was a moment's silence before her voice, that deep supple voice, answered,

"You're a very good man, you know."

3

In the corridor on the way to the courtroom, they came face to face with the German couple. The boy was not with them.

At the sight of Madeleine Clozel they halted, uncertain. The man stood stiffly, his thick shoulders drawn back, arms rigid. His wife, short and plump, in coat and skirt and a white blouse starched and ironed to a glassy smoothness, was very pleasant to look at, with her large hands, sunburned and oven-hardened, bright blue eyes, and rosy flat-boned cheeks. A smell of newly washed garments came from her. She took a step forward, and held out her hand. Madeleine Clozel ignored it, and walked past her.

She was trembling. "I couldn't," she excused herself, "I couldn't. Perhaps she didn't know what went on in the camps. And even if she knew—or knows now—no one who wasn't there knows really. And then . . . no, I couldn't—because of those who died of the hunger and the beatings. I have no right to forgive for them, have I?"

"No one blames you," Michal said gently.

A smiling irony altered her pale face. "Oh, yes, they do! Do you know what that nicely spoken young man who met us yesterday said to me at the door of the hostel? *Whatever happens tomorrow, madame, we must begin now to forgive and forget.* . . . I could have said to him: You were a French child at school then, you will never have to try to shut your eyes and ears to what rises in your mind before you can stop it, to those vacant faces, those dying bodies, those cries."

She stopped, and looked at him with an extraordinary simplicity, almost the simplicity of a little girl. "What I cannot forgive, cannot, Monsieur Michal, is that—in that place—I reached the point of not caring whether I saw my child again or not. It was only afterwards—when I came home—"

In the courtroom, he made himself as solid as possible, sitting close to her, to try to control the continual trembling of her body under its cloak. After a time it ceased.

He turned his attention to the three judges. How peculiar, he reflected, that a case concerning a French child should be in the hands of Americans. But everything nowadays is in their hands, damn it. France and the whole of Europe is being pushed aside.

He brought his mouth close to the ear of the French-speaking official on his left. "Which of them voted last time to return the boy?"

"The right-hand one. Hush."

They say, he thought ironically, that the Americans are all Germans or the grandchildren of Germans, but this one looks like a Red Indian. . . . The long sallow face, sunken dark eyes and long mouth, pleased him better than either of the other faces, one plump and good-humored, like an elderly baby, the other a block of hard heavy flesh, wider at the jowls than across the forehead, long upper lip, pale severe eyes. That's the everlasting enemy, he said to himself.

A uniformed official was reciting the bare facts of the case— briefly. None of the judges appeared to listen. It had been gone through before, thoroughly: there was nothing new, except what the boy's mother might have to say.

On the stand, she was very small, and for a time inaudible. "Try to speak up," the "Red Indian" said quietly.

She had little to answer at first except: Yes.

You were arrested with your husband on such and such a day?

Yes.

You were sent first to the farm at Neuberg, in East Prussia?

Yes.

Three more as simple questions, then:

Did you inform the authorities that you were pregnant?

No.

Did you inform your employer or his wife?

No.

Why not?

After a moment, she said:

"They could, later, see for themselves."

From where he sat, Aristide Michal saw the stretched skin of her hands folded on the rail in front of her. As the questions and answers went on, he began to see rising behind her the very small disused outhouse she slept in, alone, since the other prisoners employed were all men: no one quite knew why she had been sent to the farm and not to one of the women's camps supplying workers for a factory. Some official mistake, no doubt.

It was a derelict place, with gaps between the boards that she tried to close with straw robbed from the pile given her to lie on. And no window. The cold that winter, he reflected, must have been a separate agony. And that March evening, when her pains started, and went on through the night, in complete darkness . . . It was still not light when the child was born, and she felt over the tiny face and limbs with her hands.

Not until nine o'clock did a farm servant come to see why she had not turned out to work.

Now—Michal felt the change in his body, a sharpening of tension starting perhaps in the comfortable clean-smelling body of the German woman at the other side of the room—came the turning point in the story.

Frau Broesike visited you at once?
She came, yes.
She brought milk and a blanket?
Yes.
And you asked her to take the child?
No.
You intended to keep it with you?
I—it was mine, my child.
Did you think that you could look after it?
Not in that place.
So, you gave it to Frau Broesike?
No. I did not give him to her.

Before her husband or anyone else could check her, the German woman had got to her feet and was saying, in a gentle unhurried voice, but with the greatest assurance,

"She is not telling the truth. She said: Yes, take him, I give him to you."

"I must ask you not to interrupt," the baby-faced judge said to her, his voice as empty of emotion as his expression. Turning to the woman on the stand, he asked her:

"Can you recall exactly what you said at the time?"

"No."

"But you are sure you did not say: Take him, I give him to you?"

Madeleine Clozel was silent. Then she answered in a voice that would have been inaudible if the silence in the room had not been complete.

"Yes . . . no . . . perhaps I did."

"Try to remember," the "Red Indian" said, leaning forward.

A shocking sound, like a dog howling at night, was torn through her open mouth. "How can you know what you are doing or saying when you are as I was? That weakness. You don't know. And who is responsible? Who took me from my home? Who deported me to that place? Who is responsible for what I may have said then? Not I. *Give me the child!*"

She was tearless, but she rocked from side to side, an arm

across her eyes, the other holding her cloak round her, as if to hold together the edges of torn flesh. Michal jumped up, but an official, two officials, one a fattish troll of a woman, appeared from behind her and took her out of the room, the troll patting her shoulder as they went.

The German woman had covered her face with her hands; her husband sat staring in front of him, with a strangely dulled look, the hands planted on his knees opening and closing as if of their own volition, or as if there were something they could do about it if they were only allowed.

We have lost, Michal thought.

During the interval, he remained sitting in the courtroom, turning over in his mind phrases he might use to comfort her. If only Vincent had been able to come, he thought ruefully: he has every word in the dictionary to draw on, and the voice for it.

He noticed that the German couple did not come back into the room. Nor did Madeleine Clozel.

Nothing remained now to be got through but the judges' speeches. The first to speak, the "Red Indian," was brief and quiet; he had heard nothing today, he said, slowly, meditatively, to make him change his opinion that the child should go to his mother. The elderly baby spoke next. In a surprisingly dry voice, he said he must dissent, again, from this opinion. For three reasons. First, the unwisdom, to put it at its mildest, of removing a child from the only home he had ever known.

Second, the unanswerable argument of the boy's wish to stay with his foster parents.

"I ask myself," he said in this crackling voice, "what worth there is in a mother love which is willing to take a child by force? And what hope can this selfish mother have of overcoming the boy's hatred and resentment of her interference with his happy life?" He paused to let the interpreter turn these sentiments into curiously frigid French. Drawing from somewhere about himself an immense handkerchief, he swathed his face in it, removing from its chubby folds a layer of talc powder.

[38]

"Thirdly—and of the greatest importance—of overriding importance. How could I reconcile it with my conscience as an educated man to take this child from a well-off industrious home in a country determined to redeem its past, with all the cultural benefits he will enjoy if he remains there, and send him to a less cultivated home in a country which has given so many signs of its deep political instability? Can I as an American . . ."

Forcing himself to sit still, swallowing the stone of anger in his throat, Aristide Michal thought: They will only turn me out if I ask the fellow to tell me more about these cultural benefits. And he didn't see Madeleine Clozel after she had enjoyed them for two years.

Through the whole hearing there had been no intervention by the third judge; he had sat in his solid lightless flesh, watching Madeleine Clozel as if he were calculating what she would be worth as scrap. When he prepared to speak now, Michal felt tempted to get up and leave without waiting for the final sentence to drop from the long merciless mouth above that preposterously wide jowl.

"In reversing my previous opinion . . ."

The words passed through Michal's body like a charge of electricity, he started to get to his feet, and the lawyer jerked him back.

". . . between two good women, one a natural and the other a foster mother, the natural rights of the true mother ought to prevail . . . to balance the culture of France against the culture of Germany is not in our province in this place . . . the devotion of the child's kind foster mother . . . the love and suffering of his natural mother . . . Children are fortunately resilient. In his own country, with new friends, new lessons to be learned, he may, I believe under God he will, soon come to feel for the woman who bore him an affection at least as deep as that he now gives his German foster parents."

Baby-face had the last word. Telling the French lawyer that he could pick up his "legal prey" the next day, he added,

"You have won your case here. I hope you can justify your victory before the Judge who will, one day, deliver the final verdict on all of us. I surely hope it."

"Well, are you satisfied?" the defense lawyer asked Michal.

"All I hope," Michal said, "is that the Judge who-etc-etc will pay no attention to us for a few years and let us get on with living a little."

4

With the lawyer's help, Michal calculated the times of trains to Cannes, through Lyons. Supposing that the boy could be handed over within the next forty-eight hours by the official of the Youth Center whose disagreeable job it was to fetch him from the Broesikes' farm to the railway station, they could reach Cannes on Monday morning, very early. More likely it would be the evening. He wired Lotte to expect him then.

But it seemed that the Broesikes, since they had lost, wanted to cut short their grief and the boy's. On Saturday morning he waited with Madeleine Clozel in a room at the station, which seemed to have been hurriedly prepared for them. It was unheated, colder, he thought, than the icy streets through which they had just driven. The lawyer, who had come with them, spoke with stiff kindness to Madeleine; she cut his words short, with a glance which wavered across his face to the door and dismissed him to an infinite distance, a glance of extreme politeness and absence.

The door opened, and the German, a war cripple, limped

in, pushing a little in front of him a tall slender boy, dark-haired, dark-eyed, who might have spent the night crying and brushing his hair, so swollen were his eyelids, so neat and licked his hair.

Madeleine Clozel's breath escaped in a light gentle groan. Michal thought she was about to faint, and gripped her by the shoulder. Freeing herself, she took a step toward the boy.

"Jean!"

He looked at her fixedly, an unmoving glare, and did not speak.

Bustling forward, the lawyer seized and shook the boy's hand and spoke to him volubly in German, and received the same cold slightly mad stare.

"A frightful scene at the farm," the crippled Youth Leader whispered to Michal. He spoke French badly, and it was a moment before Michal understood him.

"He'll settle down in time."

"Let's hope," the German said roughly. "But you have something on your hands. In my opinion—"

Without waiting to hear his opinion, Michal turned to the French lawyer. "Can we go?"

"Yes. At once."

Madeleine had begun to speak to her son in halting German. She finished a phrase and began another, which ended in two or three stammered words; either she had no more German, or no more courage to persist in face of the boy's silent hostility. Lifting one hand, she was going to touch his cheek. He drew back sharply, and her arm dropped to her side. Glancing at Michal, she said in a low voice,

"The eyes and forehead are my husband's—exactly. The rest is strange."

Because they were catching an earlier train than the one expected, there were, luckily, no reporters. Very luckily, since, as the train moved off, the boy, who so far had not said one word, leaned from the window and shouted a sentence at the

Youth Leader, who grimaced and waved an arm.

"Oh, no, no, Jean, no, no, no," Madeleine Clozel said.

"What did he say?" Michal asked.

She half closed her eyes. "He said: Tell my mother and father I shall come back."

"Don't fret," Michal said. "You know—as they say—the blood speaks."

I should have asked them to send Lotte another telegram, he thought, vexed.

He had the impression, during the endless journey with its four changes of train, of being shut up in the compartment with a caged wild animal. The boy was not sullen or in any way unruly, he was ice. He sat in his seat by the window with folded hands, without speaking, his face shut. Is he always so white? Michal wondered. On the platform at Lyons, he began to walk up and down, a few yards each way, head poked forward, turning sharply as though he had come up against invisible bars. The tears began pouring down his face, and his mother started forward.

"No," Michal said, "let him alone now."

Crying will soften him, he thought. It had the contrary effect. When they were in the train again, the glance the boy turned on them was one of cold controlled hatred. In the dining car, he refused to eat, and Michal lost patience.

"Eat your food," he shouted.

For the first time, the boy answered him. "Nein, ich—ich—" Breaking off, he touched his throat.

He can't swallow, thought Michal. Seized with a useless pity for this stubborn young lunatic, he said no more.

During the night the boy slept, leaning back in his corner, jolted helplessly by the train. Even in sleep his face was shut against them, lips pressed close: a long black smudge down one cheek made him look younger than his twelve years. His mother watched him, openly now that she had not to avoid or endure his cold stare, and with a mingled joy and terror

[43]

from which Michal looked away: it had occurred to him that her face might have worn this look when she was feeling over a small body in the icy darkness of that outhouse, and after that he could not look at her. This second birth was as hard for her, in its different way, as the first, and perhaps more hopeless. Glancing at the sleeping boy, he caught himself wondering whether the baby-faced judge might not have been right.

His spirits rose again as they neared Cannes. At one moment they passed a garden full of mimosa in flower, and without thinking he drew the boy's attention to it, moving in a gentle breeze off the sea, its delicate color like a yellow fleece taking and tossing back the early light.

The boy glanced and glanced away.

Ah, to get home, Michal thought. His body, weary from the long hours in unheated trains, drew fresh energy from its thought of Lotte, at this very moment probably pushing back the bedclothes, stretching her magnificent arms, yawning, tapping the back of her hand against her teeth. The contrast between his lot and Madeleine Clozel's, between his true family and her pretense of one, was a little cruel. He pushed it out of his mind.

In the station he hesitated between waiting for the train to Grasse, taking a taxi the twenty-five-odd miles to St.-Loup, and telephoning Philippe to bring the car here. He decided on the taxi, despite the cost, because the thought of waiting here with the boy for any length of time was intolerable. Something in the rigidity, the controlled anger of this young creature, gave him an unpleasant feeling of helplessness; he did not know what to do, what to try to say to him. The boy was *not there*: to talk to him was like stepping on ground that slid away under your foot.

Poor Madeleine, he thought. But she must take what she had got. It was unjust, she had been cheated, but she had at least a very slight chance of happiness.

Beyond Grasse, the rays of the still invisible sun fanned out behind the livid amphitheater of hills. Looking at them, Michal felt full of joy; it rose through him to his throat. What a sun, he thought confusedly, what country, what a splendid life. . . . Never, he had never, even as a young man, been as happy as now. So many lives, like that of poor Madeleine, missed their mark, but his, his, went straight into the light.

For an extra tip, the driver agreed to risk his cab in the lower village. As it jolted down the narrow street, between the old houses with their shuttered windows and dark wind-corroded stone, he saw the look of dismay widening in the boy's eyes, and for a moment, standing in front of Madame Clozel's house he saw it with eyes used to the whitewashed tidiness and space of a German farm and almost felt the shock of disgust and horror in the young thin body.

For the first time since the platform at Lyons, the boy's savage self-control gave way. But this time he did not cry. Turning to Michal, he spoke a few words in a sarcastic voice, not the voice of a young boy.

"What is he saying?" asked Michal.

After a moment, Madeleine Clozel answered nearly inaudibly,

"He—he says: Am I expected to live in this place?"

Before Michal could make any effort to help her, he heard his name called. Turning, he saw that heads had been poked from windows usually, at this hour on a Sunday morning, still covered by blinds or shutters. It was Truchi who had shouted from the square before the hotel. Half running, the policeman reached him with only enough breath in his heavy body to say,

"Monsieur Michal. We didn't expect you. But thank God."

5

The evening before, possibly about the time when he was watching Jean Clozel pace the platform at Lyons like a trapped animal, two young men who had dined in the restaurant asked Lotte if they could have a bedroom for the one night. No one was staying in the hotel, and she said, Yes, certainly, and gave them the only room with a stove.

During the night, perhaps about two, but it could as easily have been midnight or four o'clock, they came into her bedroom: one held her down in bed with a hand over her mouth while the other emptied on to the floor every cupboard and drawer until he came on the keys to the safe. He emptied it of the bundles of notes, cramming them into a knapsack. Then, between them, they pushed her chemise into Lotte's mouth, tore a sheet into strips to make a rope, and fastened her to the bed by her wrists and ankles, so securely that between pain and terror she was unconscious when Philippe, getting no answer to his shouts of, "Coffee ready, Ti," opened the door of the room.

Truchi's wife and another woman were with her when Michal came in. He turned them out.

The bed was still in the middle of the room where they had dragged it to get at the safe, the curtain hiding the recess had been torn down and the door of the safe was open. He barely glanced at it.

Looking up at him, Lotte burst into tears and wept convulsively, trying to speak and only able to stammer a senseless phrase.

"Be quiet now," he said, "it's all right, I'm here, you're all right."

"But the money—the money—"

"Never mind that now."

The women had soaked strips of linen from the torn sheets in cold water and rolled them round her wrists. She began to pull at one of these bandages.

"Don't do that," he said.

"Yes, yes, I want you to see. Look what they did to me."

The wrist was badly swollen and discolored, and in one place, where the skin had been broken, there was a streak of blood. Looking at it, Michal felt the muscles at the side of his neck swell as they did in one of his accesses of rage. If, at this moment, he could have laid hands on the man who did it he would have killed him without a thought, as involuntarily as treading on a cockroach.

He heard a step behind him in the room. He turned. Philippe had come in and was staring at this bruised wrist with an indefinable expression on his face—pity? alarm? At the sight of him, Lotte's tears broke out again.

"Look, Philippe—do look what they did—they needn't have been so rough—"

The lightest of light smiles crossed Philippe's face. Bending over her, he stroked her forehead and the black clusters of hair falling round it.

"Poor Ti," he said soothingly, "never mind. It's all over, and you're safe."

"Didn't you send anyone for the doctor?" Michal asked sharply.

He had never seen her in so frightened and abject a state, and he began to think she had some more serious hurt than bruised ankles and wrists.

"Yes, of course, dad, I sent Truchi's boy off at once, but Dr. Bertin was called out during the night to, I forget where, a kid with bronchitis. His housekeeper said she'd tell him the moment he got home. Listen—isn't that him now?"

It was, arriving together, Dr. Bertin and the Police Commissioner from Grasse, with two constables. After a few words Michal left the doctor alone with her, and sat down in the café with the Commissioner while the two policemen, one a very young man with a delirious squint—how the devil did he get into the police?—waited, standing respectfully against the wall.

"What will you drink?"

"Oh," the Commissioner said, "give me a brandy, Michal, it's damnably cold still. Why do you imagine I came myself? I'll lunch here."

Fetching the brandy, and another for himself, Michal gestured toward the others. Pursing his mouth, the Commissioner shook his head violently. "Unnecessary." He swallowed his brandy, and said,

"Now!"

Michal knew him—very well. Monsieur Luc-Albert Gaudo's position in Grasse did not rest on his office: he had private means, and socially he was not only acceptable but assured of his place in political and landowning drawing rooms of the finer sort. A big man, with the head of Caligula and the body of an overfed aging ox, he dined in the restaurant twice or three times every week. He knew a great deal about food and wine, and talked readily about both. But—this was his peculiar glory —he also knew a great deal about modern literature and had written, and published at his own expense, a volume of poems which he dedicated "to Jean Cocteau, master of irony and surprises," and showed, framed in ivory and hanging on the wall of his study at home, the letter in which the poet thanked him for "this delicate attention, these gleaming feathers thrown off by an archangel who hides his wings under the uniform of a Guardian."

It was perhaps this second reputation—or ambition—which made him wish to be addressed, even when it was in the highest degree unsuitable, as Monsieur Gaudo.

He had the reputation, with his subordinates more than with his friends, of a terrible bully. On little or no provocation, a less than excellent meal, an ill-timed request, he raved at the offender in a powerful voice. This same voice, deep, flexible, vibrant, sent a shudder down the spines of his hearers when he made the speech at an official dinner party, or dedicated a belated monument to the dead of the last war, tasks it would have been absurd to hand over to a visiting politician when this magnificent instrument was at hand. A voice to turn the blood backward in your veins, people said. And if the dead heard it, they must surely turn over on their faces and put finger bones in their ears. Only to hear him saying *nos morts* was an experience no one went through unchanged.

He had a mistress he kept in decent comfort in Nice, but without failing in his attentions to a plain sickly wife, older than himself. She was very rich, an heiress, the end of an old solid family with useful offshoots, and this may have been his reason for marrying her, but he had never treated her with a less than delicate care, even tenderness. She adored him shamelessly, and was happy.

This *decent* bully Michal found likeable, more likeable than the fellow deserved, no doubt. He was not offended by the policeman's vanity, shrewdness, effrontery. On the contrary, he admired and respected a past master of certain tricks of the politician's trade.

"Who," Gaudo asked him, "knew you had this money?"

"My wife. The lawyer, Maître Jouassaint."

Gaudo rolled eyes and mouth in rather brutal geniality. "I doubt whether he hired two brigands to rob you."

It was only at this moment that the extent of his misfortune struck Michal with the force of a blow between the eyes. He gave a smothered groan. He controlled himself at once, but the whole inside of his body seemed to drop, and he could not have moved in his chair to avoid a knife aimed at him.

"Why the devil were you keeping it in the house?"

"God knows. I—I was mad."

The humiliation, the disgrace of appearing as an imbecile before his neighbors and friends, and all other sensible people, seared him. The loss of the money was a misfortune, nearly inconceivable. This other anguish was, for the moment, worse. For all their liking for him, not one of the people he saw every day would be able to repress a malicious pleasure in his loss. So little happens in St.-Loup-de-Grâce.

"It would only have been here the one night if I hadn't had to go to Frankfurt with Madame Clozel. It was because of that . . . if it hadn't been for that . . . the money would have been handed over to old Larrau next day."

"Suppose," the Commissioner said, "you tell me exactly what you did when you brought the money here that afternoon. You took it out of a bag of some sort, you—Go on, man, go on."

Speaking slowly, Michal recited the whole simple story, to the moment when, just before getting into bed, he gave Lotte his keys.

"No one else saw you put the money away?"

"No."

"Not your son? No one?"

"No one at all."

"Where did she put the keys?"

"I think, at the back of a drawer with underclothes. One of two or three drawers."

"And no one knew she had them?"

"No one. Unless she told the boy."

Gaudo leaned back in his chair, beckoning the young squinting constable, and sent him down to the kitchen in search of Philippe. When they returned, he made Philippe sit down at the table and in a smiling teasing voice said,

"Do you know what? You upset my personal secretary."

Philippe blushed hotly. "Your—?"

"A-ha. Look at him, Michal, look at your handsome son. Yes, my boy, I mean the pretty girl with the big eyes, Mademoiselle Lucile Ohrel. You paid her every sort of attention for four or five weeks, then dropped her flat. Is that a way to behave? Never mind, never mind, no doubt you had to run for your life, I know these innocent young women." Leaning forward, he tapped Philippe on the knee with two fingers of his large well-cared-for hand. "When did your mother tell you about the money in the safe?"

Philippe had recovered his calm. "I think—the day dad left. Tuesday. Tuesday afternoon. Yes. We were making out the order for me to take into Grasse, and she said: You know, I don't like the idea of all that money in my room. I asked her what money, and then she told me."

"And told you where she had put the keys."

He shook his head. "No. No, she didn't tell me that."

"And you heard nothing last night?"

"No." He spread his hands out, lifting them in one of his light gestures. "How could I? I sleep downstairs, at the other side of the restaurant. I might have heard a scream, but—poor Ti—she couldn't make a sound, let alone scream."

After a few more questions, Gaudo dismissed him, shaking a threatening finger, with another joke about his cruelty to virgins.

"You know what, Michal. With his looks he should be in Hollywood."

"God forbid."

[51]

"Well. There may be worse places. . . . Now. I shall have to talk to your wife, you know. And there is the little matter of fingermarks and so on and so on. I'll take my chaps up to the bedroom the two of them had, but first—"

"My wife is in no state to be questioned," Michal said curtly.

"We'll talk to Bertin about it." He frowned, and began to drum on the table, rapidly and noisily, with four fingers. "You know, one thing strikes me. You know what that is? How much information they had. They knew you had a lot of money here, they knew whereabouts the safe was in the room, they knew, or they could make a good guess, where to look for the keys. Interesting, eh?"

"They might," said Michal, "have known nothing more than that there *is* a safe—it's no secret. And that I was away."

"Marseilles—Nice, too, now—is full of scum—whores, pimps, Algerians and—and the rest." He had been going to say: and Greeks, and had caught the word back barely in time. There were bounds to his indifference to other people's feelings. "Ah, here is Bertin. Tell me, doctor, I can talk to Madame Michal, eh? I must!"

"I suppose it's necessary—"

Michal interrupted him. "You've examined her? Is she badly hurt?"

The doctor sat down, easing his soft dilapidated body into the chair. "My God, I'm sleepy. Why must children have all their worst crises at night? . . . No, she's not injured. Shock, bruises—nothing worse. She's splendidly built to stand a shock. Keep her in bed a day or two, she'll be as right as rain. I'll send a sedative, you can give it to her at once, and I'll look at her again this evening. . . . As for you—" he nodded at the Commissioner—"yes, you can talk to her, but make it short. I want to get home."

He stood up, groaning, and went back into the bedroom. They heard him speaking gently to Lotte, then, raising his voice, he said:

"Come in, you."

Michal followed Gaudo, and stood, halfway between the bed and the door, watching. A feeling he did not recognize for what it was churned the brandy he had poured into his empty stomach and made his hands itch to throw the two men out of his bedroom and Lotte's. The doctor remained standing near the bed, but Gaudo settled himself comfortably in the armchair, legs spread out, as if he were in his own drawing room. The fat brute, Michal said to himself: two wrong words and I'll wring his thick neck.

"Madame Michal," Gaudo said softly, "I am sorry you have had this bad time, but never mind, we shall catch these two scoundrels and make them suffer for it. I promise you. Now—just a question or two. But take your time, there's no hurry."

Lotte's nightgown, open at the base of her throat, exposed a triangle of tawny gleaming skin, moist with sweat; a lock of hair and the edges of the cotton gown clung to it. She had recovered a little of her serenity. She tried to smile at Gaudo, the grimace of a schoolgirl caught out in a silly fault.

"I—what do you want me to say?"

"These young men—they were both young, eh?—have you ever seen them here before?"

"Never."

"Describe them to me."

"I—" she ran the point of her tongue over her lips—"I hardly looked at them. They came in, and sat at the table in the corner —the one without a light. They ate the whole dinner, and they had a carafe, not a bottle, a carafe of red, and brandy with their coffee. Then they went upstairs and sat in the café and drank more brandy. Then one of them asked about a bedroom—I was a little vexed—the nuisance, you know, when we were short-handed. But I sent the old woman—Thérèse Lemice, you know, who helps with the washing-up—to make up the beds, and—and that was that."

"It was you who waited on them? Not Philippe?"

[53]

She moved her head on the pillow. "Philippe doesn't like to serve. Besides, he was cooking. He was in the kitchen all evening."

Gaudo leaned forward, hands planted on his broad knees. "Well, now, you must have noticed something about them when they spoke to you. Some little thing. Did they, let's say, speak pleasantly? What color was their hair? Did you see a mark on either of their faces? A mole? A mustache? A scratch?"

"No." She smiled faintly. "Perhaps I'm peculiar, I never look at the customers. Except, I mean, to see if they have finished, or if they want something. I look at their plates or their glasses—and their hands."

"Ah. And these two fellows' hands, what were they like?"

"One of them had very long fingers," she said after a moment.

From where he stood, Michal could see a trickle of moisture, starting at her temple, run slowly down her cheek and the side of her throat. He made a movement which caught Gaudo's eye. The Commissioner smiled and said amiably,

"Your husband thinks I am tormenting you, eh?"

The blood rose to Michal's head. "You could cut this a little shorter."

"One minute, one more minute. Don't you want to get to the bottom of this business? You want your money back, you want me to catch the rascals, don't you?"

"I want you out of here," Michal growled.

"A minute," Gaudo repeated. He let his body sink back in the chair, as though the interrogation were becoming unimportant, a simple gossip between friends. "My dear Madame Michal, one more question. When did you tell your son that there was all this infernal money in the safe?"

"Philippe?" She opened her eyes widely, fixing them on him with an air of astonishment, or it might have been resentment. "I told him some time on Friday. Or Saturday itself. Yes, Saturday."

"Ah," Gaudo said gently, "Philippe said it was Tuesday afternoon."

Still fixed on him, her eyes filled slowly with tears. "It could have been Tuesday. I don't think it was. I forget. My head aches, I can't think any more."

Michal took two steps to the side of the armchair, near enough to Gaudo to catch his powerful smell of cigars, toilet water, brandy. But before he could speak, the doctor had intervened.

"I think that's enough."

"I should damned well think so," Michal said violently. "Out with you. Both of you. Leave her alone."

"Michal," said the doctor, "you don't imagine I waited here for nothing, for the pleasure of listening to our friend's fine voice? No harm has been done your wife, she needs to sleep now, she needs a day or two in bed—but that's all, I assure you. If there are any more questions, I daresay they can wait a day or two—or three—"

"Yes, yes," Gaudo interrupted. His face was so broad that it had room for more than one expression at a time. At the moment his mouth smiled genially while his savage little eyes were taking in every detail of the room, with ferocious absorption, from the door of the safe swinging open and the closed cupboards and drawers, to the woman lying in the bed. The glance he sent over her face, over firmly, sensuously rounded forehead, eyelids, chin, was as hectoring as that he gave the room, and quite as impersonal.

"Who tidied up the room?" he said suddenly.

"Madame Truchi. Thérèse," Lotte said.

"And left their sweaty trail everywhere." Scowling, he dragged himself up. "I hope at least they didn't lay hands on that—" He jerked his arm at the safe. "We'll see to it now, before we go upstairs."

Michal thrust his head forward. "You'll what?"

"Michal," the doctor said.

"It strikes me," Gaudo said, grinning, "that what we need here is two sedatives."

Straddling his legs, he went to the door, and beckoned the young constable, who came in averting his eyes from the bed. But with that squint, he might actually have been looking straight at it.

Controlling himself with an effort he felt in the joints of arms and back, Michal leaned against the wall and stood there, waiting. Nothing moved in his heavy face except his deep-set eyes, which followed every move made by the three policemen.

During the afternoon he got a message from the schoolmaster, asking him to come to the mairie at four o'clock.

In his capacity as secretary of the mairie, Blaise Vincent sat in his office there every day for two or three hours after four o'clock, when he closed the school for the day. He had less than a hundred yards to walk from the schoolhouse immediately behind the mairie, at the other side of a small graveled courtyard. His own house, with its scrap of kitchen garden, faced this courtyard: its windows had no other outlook, and when his wife was alive they were shrouded by thick muslin curtains, to protect her and her family from the spectacle of the children when they were galloping about the yard, and their prying glances. But they cut off the light, too, and after she died Vincent stripped bare the three upstairs windows; these rooms were bedrooms, little used during school hours. Every window had its outside shutter of old blistered wood.

The mairie, a single-story building, faced the square. Vincent's office behind the shabby council room with its discolored flag and bust of Marianne had a tiled floor and a stove which gave out more fumes than heat, so that he had to keep the window open a few inches even in the worst cold. In 1940 a shell splinter had penetrated to a lung, and for all his friend Bertin could do to ease him he spent the winter coughing, his small yellow face, as lively as a monkey's and with a monkey's sorrowful charm, crumpled like a rag.

With Aristide Michal he carried on an endless and on the whole good-tempered feud. Every document on which he put the mairie stamp—pensions, health insurance, family allowances—had been scrutinized and verified, to make certain that no creature, man or woman, got a farthing to which he was not fully entitled. Not because he was a skinflint—on the contrary, he suffered from chronic generosity—but because, to him, the vacant-eyed bust in the council room was that of a virgin goddess, to be served in total honesty. As blindly and faithfully as he loathed the Catholic Church, he worshiped in a church he had invented—apparently without noticing how many different assumptions his Republican virgin had survived.

The deputy mayor's readiness to countersign papers and letters he knew to be false—at best, imperfectly honest—if it were a little matter of getting something out of the government for any inhabitant of St.-Loup-de-Grâce, shocked him to the heart. Waving his arms, coughing, he jumped up and down in front of Michal's solid body each time it happened, like, Michal told him calmly, a monkey on a stick—and to as much purpose.

When Michal came in he stood up quickly, and held out both hands, trembling with emotion and cold.

"What abominable luck. My dear fellow, I have no words."

"They're not called for," Michal said. "It was my fault entirely, I shouldn't have had the money there."

"Oh. If all our follies were punished . . . What will happen now?"

Michal shrugged. "Our Monsieur Gaudo was about the place for more than five hours—counting the time he spent over lunch. He seems to think he can do something."

"Gaudo? Extraordinary man. A monster of vanity and egoism."

"He's not abnormal. Simply franker than most of us—and more successful."

"Tell me—before I confess why I brought you here—something about the Clozel boy. His mother is bringing him to see me this evening. I can tell you, I'm not happy about it. How the devil am I to fit a young Boche into the school? And what's going to become of him? I don't teach saints."

"He didn't want to come."

"I gathered that. But—God damn it—she has a right to him."

"And you think that's going to help her?"

"She gave him his life, she suffered hell in that place. She's owed something."

"Who owes her?" Michal said. "Listen. That's the purest twaddle. We're in life like being in the open air or a thunderstorm. It's a state, a condition. Nothing in it implies that Madeleine Clozel will be consoled because she's been cruelly treated. She may be. But she'll have to take what she gets. Like everyone else." He grinned. "Like me."

"I hope," Vincent said slyly, "that this time you'll get off better than you deserve."

Michal laughed. "Since I don't believe in justice—or injustice—perhaps I shall. Why did you want to see me?"

The other fidgeted a little. "Admit that I'm not in the habit of interfering."

"What have you been doing?"

"It happened that this morning, after morning school, I had an appointment with Larrau, here, about the compensation for his barn—to which he's not my God entitled—and I asked him what he was going to do if you couldn't buy the hotel. He said he hadn't made up his mind."

"Well?"

Vincent had a fit of coughing. When he emerged from it, face distorted, eyes streaming tears, he said,

"I asked him to come in here this afternoon and talk it over with you. He agreed. Are you vexed?"

"No," Michal said coldly. Suddenly he crashed both fists on the desk. "God help me, every man, woman and child in the place is laughing at me for a crazy idiot. Why should I mind

Paul Larrau? Let him insult me. I can stand it."

"Aristide," the schoolmaster said, using the other's Christian name for the first time in their lives, and perhaps the last, "you are not a vain man, and you know precisely what you are worth—"

"No one," interrupted Michal, grinning, "can prepare a *truite farcie* or a *pain d'écrivisses* to beat mine. And I can outtalk the devil."

"—then why do you care so much what people feel about you?"

"I don't. Whether I'm liked or disliked matters less to me than a fine day. But—admit it—there is a certain human dignity no one likes to forfeit. I don't like the spectacle of myself as an imbecile."

Vincent stood up. "Here he comes."

Nothing in Paul Larrau's expression when he came into the room gave away his pleasure in being in a position to force another man to dance to his humor. He sat down, making a ceremony of rubbing his small hands to warm them, relighting a half-smoked cigarette at which he sucked toothlessly, crossing his bony knees, and said in a placid voice,

"Well, Monsieur Michal, I take it you haven't brought me any money."

"No. It's gone. For the time at least."

"Ah, ah! What do you propose to do?"

Michal looked at him without a change of expression. "Nothing. It's up to you."

The old fellow's eyes sparkled. "In my skin what would you do?"

"I can't imagine myself in your skin."

Larrau gave his horrible laugh. "Don't get it into your head that I respect you any better for going off to Germany, on an errand of mercy, as they say. You're a sentimentalist. I'm not. In fact, I can't think why you did it. Only a simpleton does things against his own interests and you're not a simpleton. You had a motive of some sort, but what it was beats me. Oh, I'm not asking you to explain yourself, all I have to say to you is: Ask yourself whether, because you behaved recklessly, I ought to. Go on, answer. Don't muzzle yourself. Why should you? I don't. Tell me to my face that I'm a greedy peasant, a bloodsucker. It won't hurt me."

More mystified than irritated, Michal said,

"If you're determined to sell the place, sell it—to the Parisian. But since you don't need the money—do you?—why not let things go on as they were before he turned up? I pay you a fair rent. What more do you need?"

"Need? I can't live in two houses at once. So—I don't need the one I rent you. But I always need land. You don't understand that, you."

Michal stood up to go. "Tell your Parisian he can have it."

"Wait a minute!" Larrau said coolly. "You may recover your money, or enough of it. I'm not in such a desperate hurry as you seem to be. I'll wait—let me see, I'll wait for three months. For good measure, I'll wait until the end of June." He leaned across the desk, and tapped Vincent on the arm. "Eh, Monsieur Vincent? What do you say?"

"I say that you are behaving generously," Vincent said warmly, all smiles.

"You talk like a fool," retorted Larrau. "I'm neither generous nor unreasonable. It suits me to wait a few months—that's all. I have nothing against our friend, and no wish to injure him. On the other hand, I don't care what happens to him or, come to that, to anyone. At my age you know very well what you want. Come to that, I never, at any age, cared about other people—they care too much about themselves! If it's a question of pulling you or my black bitch out of the river I know which I'd choose."

He laughed.

"I'm much obliged," Michal said. To get his money back he could not have added a word.

Outside, in the half-light, he drew a long breath of the razor-sharp air, trying to shake off a giddiness half excitement, half anger. Nothing worse than this will ever happen to me, he thought. But if it does, well, I can stand it.

As he passed Madame Clozel's house, he glanced toward the upper window, and saw a pale blur he took to be the boy's face pressed to the glass. It vanished at once.

Outside the hotel he stood for a minute leaning on the low wall, staring down between the black stones and derelict olive trees into the vast snake pit of whorled rocks and planes sinking toward the sea. Directly ahead of him, a narrow corridor opened in the sky, full, like a pomegranate, of seeds. A sudden wild exhilaration seized him.

It's going to be all right, he thought.

He turned to go in. Madame Truchi, opening the side door to throw out a little water from a bowl, saw the triumphant look on his face, and thought: Ah, good! He's heard something about the brigands.

6

A month later, in the last week of April, he had still not heard. From the moment the two men, leaving Lotte helpless in her room, walked out of the hotel in the darkness and got into their car, they disappeared. No one was able to describe even the car, which one of the men had put away in the shed before dining: and before that, it had passed unremarked through a village used to seeing small cars jolt down the steep street on their way to the hotel. Gaudo was making no bones about the surprise and disgust with which his discomfiture filled him. A crime he had seen at first as so simple, almost puerile, as to be barely interesting—except that the victim was a man who should have known better—was making him look an incompetent fool. All the more exasperating in that it was clearly an amateur affair, in which none of the professional Riviera thieves well known to him and his colleagues along the coast, and regarded by them almost indulgently as fellow craftsmen, was involved. He suffered tortures of nervous indigestion. What his subordinates had to suffer only they and their families knew.

George Leighton had been kept at home after a fall which cracked four of his brittle ribs and fractured a wrist. He was dining in the restaurant for the first time since the robbery. To celebrate his recovery, Michal had cooked a dinner which only an insensitive man could eat except in silence.

Not that he had any need to disturb his enjoyment by asking questions: the doctor had been keeping him informed, daily, about the progress—the lack of progress—of the police in their efforts to trace the thieves. Toward the end of the meal, when he congratulated Michal on it, he asked,

"Nothing has been heard yet of your money?"

"Nothing," Michal said. His easy laughter rolled out. "They say that Monsieur Gaudo has dyspepsia, hardened arteries, and the beginnings of renal disease. He hasn't been here for a week."

"You're not worrying, then?"

"What good would it do me? If I've only three months to live I'd be a fool to spoil them by worrying."

"True," Leighton said.

He watched Michal move about the room with his quick indolent-seeming movements. A less indolent man did not exist. The unquenchable energy and gaiety of his mind sprang like the jet of a fountain from a physical gusto which barely needed sleep to renew itself. For less than a moment Leighton had an impulse to lend him the money he needed to save himself. It would straiten him somewhat, but he could at a pinch do it.

Shall I? he thought. No. . . . He had an ineradicable dislike of involving himself with any man to the extent of doing him a considerable service. Gratitude, if he got it, would only irritate him, and in fact he did not believe that gratitude is a normal human feeling. Animals are often grateful, men rarely. He felt a genuine liking for the Greek—but it was not so strong as his indifference.

I used to be more generous, he thought coolly. Not any more, I'm too old, too tired. It would only be a nuisance to see him every day, in the relation of debtor to benefactor.

He knew one thing. Aristide Michal would not ask him for a loan. His politeness and friendliness were natural qualities, not a manner he had practiced, not commercial, but the nature itself was ungovernable. When he stood, smilingly attentive, taking some well-to-do man's orders, he did it as an equal. To ask for a gift—gift or loan, what was the difference?—was impossible to him. He had never made advances toward anyone. It was his clients, it was the villagers, who made the advances, not he.

In the café that evening the circle was complete for the first time since the Englishman had his accident, and even old Larrau showed his satisfaction by ordering for himself a second glass of the rough wine he drank.

Coming in a little later than the others, Pibourdin was egg-full of mischief. He began by asking Michal, with an unspeakably discreet air of concern, if it were true that the police had sent for Philippe to question him about the two men he, Pibourdin, had seen with him in Nice only a few evenings before the robbery.

"Until a week ago," Michal said calmly, "Monsieur Gaudo was here every other day, asking questions of everyone who has ever been inside the house for longer than ten minutes. When he could think of nothing else, he asked old Thérèse what was the last thing she did at night before leaving the hotel to go home. She told him: the same she did in the morning at five o'clock when she got up and went outside, at the back of her own house."

"Then Philippe was not sent for to be questioned by the police at Grasse?"

"Philippe? Yes. And myself, and my wife—three or four times—and even Truchi's boy, who was so alarmed that his father had to take him there by the back of his neck, like a kitten."

"What," asked Leighton, "are the police now looking for?"

"Still the same thing," Michal said. He laughed. "All the money I have in the world, bar four weeks' takings . . . What they believe now, I gather, is that, in all probability, the two fellows were only expecting to pick up what was in the till, here, and any money or anything of value my wife might have in the bedroom with her: they had no idea of such a killing."

"But they knew enough to go straight to her room," Pibourdin said, smiling. "And they knew where it was. Who could have told them?"

"You. Anybody. Any one of you. Or they noticed it for themselves."

Larrau let out his scream. "None of us is above suspicion. And no one. The only way, the only sane way, to live is to trust no one, neither your wife, nor your children, nor friends— not one of them is incapable of making a fool of you. And why? Why do they do it? Because."

Pibourdin asked slyly,

"Did your wife ever make a fool of you?"

"Judging her by other women," Larrau said, eying him as though he knew some ludicrous secret, "yes. And more than once."

"Monsieur Larrau," Leighton said coolly, "you are a man after my own heart, but this conversation bores me. It quarrels with my dinner."

"Oh. As you like, as you like."

"The dinner I have just eaten," Leighton went on, "was in its way as magnificent as—" he paused and addressed himself to the schoolmaster—"as the *Iliad* or any other masterpiece of writing or a great painting or a symphony by Mozart. I should like to know what part of his brain a man uses to produce a masterpiece, including a masterly dinner."

"Why only his brain?" Vincent began. He started to cough, and coughed himself nearly speechless. "If you ask me," he whispered, "he can create with any part of his anatomy. It's a question of degree—or habit."

"With his spleen?" asked Leighton.

"Why not with his spleen?"

Michal laughed. "Let me tell you something. At different times, I cook with a different tool. With my fingers one day, with my brain, with my memory. This evening, for example,

I cooked with a part of my body I should need to start a family."

"Good. I believe you," Leighton said.

It was a fine light evening, almost warm. More people were coming into the café than for several weeks, "old nanny goat" had more to do than she could do easily, and Michal spent the next hour behind the bar. When he returned to the circle, the time was after eleven, Pibourdin and old Larrau had both gone, and the doctor was trying to coax Vincent to leave with him. So long as they were sober, these two men in their fifties were like schoolboys together, sharing foolish jokes, nudging each other in the ribs, chuckling. The doctor had a head of iron, but invariably a moment came when Vincent was as likely to quarrel or weep as laugh—or start a paroxysm which never ended.

"Either we go now," Bertin was saying, "or I won't be responsible for getting you home safely."

"Right, I'm quite ready."

"Then come."

Vincent did not move. Scowling at Michal, he said, "What is this I hear about that rascal Cabrot and his pension?"

"Who told you about it?"

"Pibourdin."

"Why do you pay any attention to that spiteful old woman?"

"Because sometimes what he tells is the truth. Did you or did you not sign a letter for him to the Minister, saying that he ruptured himself putting out a fire, when we all know, Félix here knows, that he did it falling off his own ladder when he was blind tight? You're an embezzler, an impostor, you—you politician!"

It was only when he had drink in him that the almost affectionate sparring between the secretary of the mairie and the deputy mayor turned sour. Michal knew better than to lose his temper. He said mildly,

"Since 1939 Cabrot has had nothing but bad luck. A prisoner, good-for-nothing sons, a whore of a wife. If he buys a

[66]

secondhand van it falls to pieces. Nothing goes right for him. There are men like that."

"No reason," Vincent said, "for playing your shifty tricks on the government."

"Come," the doctor said sternly. "Get up. Walk."

Vincent came unsteadily to attention. "Sir!"

They went out arm in arm. Watching them go, Leighton said, brusquely,

"Sit down a minute. Tell me—what will happen if you don't recover your money? What will Larrau do?"

"Sell to the Parisian. If he had never been offered the money he would have been perfectly content with what I pay him. But he has already, in his head, laid the money out on land, sheep, a new barn, the rest, and he couldn't now endure not getting it."

"How long have you had the place?"

"Twenty-seven years. I've had three leases from him, at three rents. The third runs out this June."

Leighton was silent for a time. In the crude light falling on him directly he looked frailer, more emaciated, than before his accident. The hands folded on the edge of the table were purely bone, the skin clinging to the joints. His great beaked nose had devoured more of his face, now completely colorless, even to the eyes, unswerving in their cold stare. He turned it on Michal.

"You came to France from Greece when you were—how old?"

"Six. I came with an uncle, my mother's brother, from a village—Langadhia. I wasn't born there, I was born in Athens. For all I know of Athens I never saw it. My father, John Michalopoulos—queer, there are moments when I can't even spell that—was a small shopkeeper, he sold guns, sporting guns. When my mother died—a week or so after I was born, her first child—he took me to her village, for her own family to bring up. After that I never saw him, I don't know when he died, or how. Langadhia I remember—a little. I remember it as like, not entirely like, this. A poor village in Akhadia, very difficult country, near the border into Elis." Throwing back his head, he laughed. "They say in Greece: All the Greek politicians come from Langadhia. . . . Desperate crafty wheedling hard-bargaining peasants. If Blaise Vincent heard that! . . . My uncle had no bent for politics. He was still a young man when he decided to try his luck in France, in Marseilles. I suppose he was about eighteen when my father handed me to him done up like a parcel in a black shawl; he took on himself to treat me as his son, and when he left Greece he didn't want to leave me behind. He was consumptive. He died in Marseilles before I was twenty, but by that time I was on my own feet."

"This place," Leighton said slowly, "I'm talking about the restaurant, is an achievement—remarkable. Created from nothing. From a Greek village, by a penniless Greek."

"Oh, as to that! Either you have your wits about you in Langadhia, or you don't survive. Is it any different here? It's a fact I mislaid mine when I went off to Frankfurt, leaving the money behind. If that devil Larrau was willing to wait, it wouldn't take me fifteen years to save it again."

A curious emotion hung between them in the air, born of the knowledge both men had that, if he chose to do it, the Englishman could lend the money. Why, Jouassaint had said, don't you try him? If you got only half of the total sum out of him, the bank would advance the rest.

The offer was not made. Michal recognized the look on Leighton's face, the harsh skepticism and amusement, almost delight, with which he viewed the antics of a man or woman in the grip of a passion—no lack of these in St.-Loup-de-Grâce, where isolation, poverty, surplus energy, can transform an inheritance of a couple of chairs and a bed into a thirty years' war. He would never lend money to enable his friend Aristide Michal to satisfy his own passion by feeding Larrau's raging greed for land and more land.

Michal felt no resentment, not a trace. He never expected, of friendship, more than a modest return. Others of his expectations were quite monstrous—all those which had to do with Philippe, for example.

"How is your wrist?" he asked. "Can you use it now to write?"

"Yes," Leighton said. He smiled mockingly. "I realize, from what you said just now about the creation of a superb dinner, that it's too late in life for me to think of producing a masterpiece."

At this moment Philippe came into the café, from the kitchen. He had pulled an old sweater over his working blues, and was going outside, he said, for a breath of cool air after the hours downstairs.

"Going far?" asked Michal.

"No, dad. Only a stroll."

He stood for a moment, looking at them with a slight smile, then walked quickly out.

Unbearable, Leighton said to himself, that he should age. That a quite flawless beauty should be destroyed, wiped out as if it had never existed, by time and all the commonness of life, marrying, working, producing children.

"What are you going to do with him?" he asked.

"In two years—three at most—I shall have taught him all I know, and passed into him all my tricks. Then I shall send him to Paris or New York—depending on the state of the world. In New York he would in due course make a great deal of money, but America"—he was thinking of the judge with the face of an elderly baby—"is an unenlightened country. Well, we shall see."

"Will he enjoy being a chef?"

Michal looked at him with frank astonishment. "Why not?"

"I must go home," Leighton said. "Where's Ahmed?"

He knew without turning his head that the Arab was sitting where he always sat during the hours his employer spent in the

[69]

restaurant and the café, perched, his back against the wall, on a stool he wedged in the narrow space at the end of the bar farthest away from the door. He hated drafts. There, with only a glass of coffee, he waited, his eyes blank, as though turned inward, in complete silence.

He came forward now and placed his fine abnormally long hands one under each of Leighton's elbows, levering him to his feet. The look on his dark face was one of blind absorption, as though he were accomplishing a rite, or as though a mother were holding in her hands a first-born son. It was almost fatuous in its intensity.

What, Michal wondered briefly, were their relations thirty years ago, when Ahmed was, let's say, sixteen?

"Ah," Leighton said, steadying himself, "I had forgotten. Madame Clozel came to see me this afternoon. She is in trouble over that boy—as she might have expected. She asked me if I would talk to him. Why she supposes that I can do anything with a rebel of—how old is he? twelve?—only she knows. But I told her I would. I thought it might be a sensible idea to talk to Vincent about him first—find out how he does at school, and what Vincent thinks about him. I also thought that you might come with me—at least to see Vincent. Your views on a twelve-year-old boy are obviously worth more than mine. Can you come?"

"Of course. Tomorrow?"

"Yes. I'll send a message to Vincent to expect us at his house after school. I refuse to freeze to death in the mairie. You don't mind seeing him?"

"On the contrary," Michal said, smiling. "Every time Monsieur Vincent insults me he needs a few hours, say twelve, to reach the right degree of repentance, neither sentimental nor querulous. I'll come."

7

Michal reached the schoolmaster's house just as Leighton's car turned into the square. He waited, and they entered the house together. It was Vincent's sister who let them in. Her brother, she told them, was still at the school; she showed them into the little sitting room, and stood there for a moment, ill at ease, her gaunt body in its holland overall rigid with anxiety to pay enough respect to the Englishman without overdoing it where Aristide Michal was concerned. When she moved, a mingled odor of camphor and cough lozenges came from her.

This room, like the whole house since she came to live here after her sister-in-law's death, was painfully clean and cold. Everything in it had been infected by her overwhelming sense of duty: the two sets of curtains, brown chenille and white starched muslin, the two armchairs only freed from their striped percale covers when a visitor was expected, the clock in the form of the Arc de Triomphe, the looking-glass with the eagles, the table of polished walnut, all opposed an unseeing parade-ground stare to what little light forced its way into the room.

"You have come to discuss the Clozel boy with my brother?"

"We have," answered Leighton.

She half closed her eyes. "A devil," she said gently, "a young Satan. That poor Madame Clozel. But what was she about to bring him here? She ought to have accepted God's will . . . Ah, here is my brother."

She escaped with relief. When Vincent came in, he walked directly to Michal and shook his hand, with a trustingly sweet smile.

"I'm told, Félix tells me, that last night I insulted you. Is it true?"

"Not a word of truth in it," Michal said.

"I'm very glad, but . . . the fact is, I ought not to drink. I don't know why I do it except that it makes me happy and I sleep very well afterward."

Michal laughed. "If you can think of a better reason," he said.

A gleam of joy crossed Vincent's small face. "One thing is certain. So long as I can count on two or three hours in every day without any sense of time or any need to watch my tongue, I have nothing to grumble about. I could live forever. Fortunately, I shan't be asked to. . . . You want to hear about Jean Clozel. Well—he's a problem, one I haven't mastered. I can tell you, there are times when I wonder whether I have the faintest idea what I'm doing with him. Only yesterday, he stood in front of me after school, with a face of stone, his eyes moving in and out of it like two snakes, and said: Damn you, I won't . . . To me, his headmaster! Damn you, he said."

"What did you do?" asked Leighton.

"Nothing. I thought: Possibly you ought to thrash him. Possibly a good thrashing is what he needs. But, you know—I may be a weak ass, but I could no more set about him than I could thrash a horse, though I've seen horses thrashed into behaving themselves and there may well have been no other way of breaking them in, but . . . in the first place I'm not sure that I want to break young Clozel, and secondly, what, when he broke, should I have on my hands? A mental case? A sick maimed child?" He shook his head. "No, no, I'm baffled."

"Does he make a habit of swearing at people?"

"No. One of the most remarkable—and remarkably disquieting —things about him is his abnormal self-control. It's unchildlike. If I thought he was simply being prudent . . . he's not prudent, otherwise he would hardly reserve these very occasional outbursts of fury for me, of all people."

"Perhaps he trusts you not to retaliate," Leighton said, with his sharp smile.

"Not a bit of it. He trusts no one. That's natural."

"How does he get on with other boys?"

Vincent pulled a saturnine face. "My God, you know what the young are like. I have thirty children in the school, girls and boys, starting at six and staying until they're fourteen or fifteen —the fourteens and fifteens, most of them, are *adults,* with all the capacity for mischief, the malice, not to say the brutality, of men and women, peasants, who know nothing about the world except that it is a hard, often boring place. I can't help knowing that, at least sometimes, they treat Jean Clozel to a foretaste of hell. It's partly his own fault. He makes no secret of his contempt for them and their barbaric ways. He has an extremely sharp tongue, and—already, in one month—enough French to make himself plain. Plain enough—too plain."

"Then he's intelligent?"

"Too intelligent for his good," Vincent said dryly.

"He works hard, does he?"

"At certain things. He won't stick at what bores him. My impression," Vincent said, grinning, "is that he has worked at the language only to be able to use his tongue. Oh, and to shake off the feeling of inferiority it no doubt gave him to hear these savages he despises speaking a language he didn't understand. I have a few words of German. When I try them on him, either he doesn't answer or he looks at me with a perfectly obvious mockery, as if he were saying: Don't think you can get round

[73]

me that way. . . . If he were less self-controlled, less ferociously shut against attempts to talk to him on any reasonable basis— he's possessed, I mean, by a kind of coldly reasoned *un*reason— yes, possessed is the word—I might not be at such a loss. It's humiliating, but I think he will have to work through his . . . his unreason, in his own way. Whether he can—ah, that's another matter. But I don't seem able to do better than nothing."

"That may," Leighton said coolly, "be the greatest kindness you can do him. I remember at my own school, one of our great public schools, there was a boy of thirteen who must, I realized later, have been going through some such crisis as this boy. He was thrashed into idiocy. And I mean idiocy."

Vincent gave him a quizzical glance. "We all know that your countrymen hate to be defeated."

Michal asked,

"Has he made any friends in the school?"

"One," Vincent said. He frowned, locking together his feminine-looking hands and dragging on them until the knuckles cracked, as he did when he was feeling uneasy. "Would you believe it?—my daughter. Yes, Marthe. I don't know what started it, because—when I noticed them together in the yard, one day after morning school, they were already very friendly. I asked Marthe a question or two, but—you know children—all she did was smile at me and say: He's quite nice really. . . . I don't care to press her. If her mother were alive. My sister—" he sighed—"my sister is a *good* woman."

"What does your sister say about it?" Leighton asked delicately.

"Oh, that no good will come of it, you can't yoke a lamb and a wolf, and so on and so forth. My instinct is that Marthe is in no danger—of any sort. At eleven, she's already self-possessed; she was always gay and good-tempered, even as a baby. Besides—" he looked at them under his glasses, with sly self-mockery— "as the schoolmaster's child, she has a certain immunity, none of the others cares to attack her for giving aid and comfort to the enemy. In fact, she's his only chance."

"You are doing the right thing," Leighton said.

"Wrong or right, I see nothing else I can do. We—all three of us, we helped Madeleine Clozel to get him back. We may have committed a crime."

"No," Michal said.

Leighton looked at him with affectionate derision. "Very probably *yes*. Nothing like putting your trust in *natural rights* to be rewarded by every sort of betrayal, heartache, wickedness. I'll go further and say that the only, yes, the only rights it is safe to exercise are those other people are afraid to deny you, because they fear you, a little or much. With those, you can be safe— even, if that amuses you, generous. Madame Clozel's rights to her son were of the wrong sort."

"You are a cynic," Vincent said, smiling.

"No. But I have lived a long time."

On their way out they saw the little Vincent girl, Marthe. She was standing in the small vegetable garden of the house, with a handful of parsley, and ran, smiling, to open the gate for them. An attractive, not a pretty child, with a sensible sweet face, ripe cheeks, very bright dark eyes, dark straight hair cut short into her neck. Michal spoke to her, and she answered him readily, looking into his face with a frankness which made her seem very charming.

"No doubt her father is right," said Michal, "she's too candid to come to any harm."

Leighton gave him a speculative glance, stretching his mouth into a line of bitter precision, but did not speak.

Outside Madame Clozel's house, Michal said,

"If you don't mind, I'll let you go in alone. You'll manage him more easily without me. Two of us at him at once—a boy who detests and mistrusts everyone—the worst possible tactics."

Ahmed had followed them from the square, a few paces behind. He would wait, blotted against the wall of the house, until Leighton came out, to support him up the street to the car.

"Very well."

Madame Clozel must have been waiting in her window, behind the curtain. Before Leighton could knock she had opened the door and drawn him across the narrow stone-tiled entry into the downstairs room. Here, he saw at once, was where she slept; the room was as tidy and as neutral as a schoolgirl's in a strict boarding school, a narrow bed, two chairs, a table with her sewing machine, a stove. The only objects which surprised him were laid on a shelf above the stove: they were a pipe, a dozen or so bound volumes of (so far as he could see) Stendhal, Baudelaire, Gide, and a man's wrist watch.

Following his glance, Madeleine Clozel said, smiling,

"My husband's. A neighbor where we lived in Paris took them from the apartment and kept them for me. They're all I have from that time. I thought—well, I always thought our son would have them."

"Where is the boy?" Leighton asked.

He had no wish to become involved in emotional details about her life. Cruelty—the sort of cruelty in which she had been trapped—revolted him, and he preferred, when he could, not to think about it. He believed that human nature is incurable: the best one can hope for is a temporary convalescence after some more than usually severe access of fever.

"In his room. Upstairs. I only have the two rooms. This one I meant to be our living room during the day, but he prefers to sit in his own."

She spoke calmly, as if she were trying to give him directions before sending him forward, and he began to feel a certain confidence in her, in her sense of propriety.

"You find him . . . unfriendly?"

She was sitting upright in the less comfortable of the two chairs, her hands in her lap, her eyes, with their absent gaze, fixed on he had no idea what point in the desert she lived in when she was alone. A faint smile crossed her face.

"Unfriendly? Yes, I suppose so. He has been with me now almost five weeks. During this time he has never *begun* a conversation. When I say something, he answers me. In the fewest possible number of words. That's all." Her smile sharpened. "In five weeks."

"He's unmanageable—is that what you're telling me?"

For the first time a little color came into her face. "Monsieur Leighton, I have not tried to manage him—if you mean by that, have I scolded him, or pleaded with him to notice me, or cried in front of him." She looked at him with a touch of defiance—almost a young defiance. And after all, he reflected, she is not more than thirty-six or seven. "In that place, I lost the habit of crying."

"The camp? Have you talked to him about it?"

"No." A tide of blood rose in her face. "That is, I tried—once. He said: *I had nothing to do with such places.*"

"Is he—does he look like his father?"

"The upper part of his face—his forehead, his eyes. And, it is very queer, very—very disturbing—he has certain gestures he makes, a way of moving his fingers, and the way he falls asleep, doubling a hand under his cheek—I have seen it once—which are his father's, exactly. That seems to me very strange, you wouldn't expect such absurd tricks to be passed down. You'll think me foolish, but they are as if my husband were making signs to me now and again."

Is she a little cracked? Leighton wondered. But her glance was livelier than usual, and there was a hint of gaiety in her voice. It struck him that the girl who had been amused or touched by her husband's way of falling asleep was not, not yet, completely out of reach. If there were anyone interested enough to stretch out a hand.

"What do you want me to say to him?" he asked gently.

"I don't know. I only thought—if you talked to him—you're not French—you might be able to persuade him that he's not living among savages. I—" she hesitated, and said with a curious dry mockery—"I don't regret fighting to get him back. What I regret is that I survived. No, no, I'm lying, in the camp I struggled to live, and lived. I wanted to have Jean with me and I have

him. Only—I deceived myself about my powers of charming a
boy of twelve. They don't exist."

"Let me see him."

She got up and went into the kitchen. It opened directly from
her room, and he caught a glimpse of a white-scrubbed table
and a dresser. Standing at the bottom of the flight of stone steps
built against the wall and disappearing behind the chimney, she
called,

"Jean."

There was a moment's silence, before he answered politely,
"Yes, Madame Clozel?"

She made a tiny grimace. She is used to it, Leighton thought,
but not to hearing him say it in front of other people.

"Will you come downstairs? Monsieur Leighton is here."

She came back into the living room and took her cloak from
a cupboard in a narrow recess of the rough limewashed walls.

"I'll leave him with you. If I stay—it would be useless. Besides, they expect me at the hotel, to look over the bed linen."

She was still in the room when the boy came in from the
kitchen. She smiled at him and said calmly,

"Monsieur Leighton has taken the trouble to come here because he is interested in you. He can . . . advise you. Better
than anyone here."

Moving quickly, she was out of the room and the house before
the boy had time to answer, if he meant to.

"Sit down," Leighton said. "This is not an interrogation."

He scrutinized the boy, wondering whether, when he arrived,
he had been as pale. His skin had a yellowish tinge. Otherwise
he was rather better than passably good-looking, well-made, tall
for his age, with fine chestnut-brown eyes under black eyebrows.
He had a pleasant voice.

"But I think Madame Clozel asked you to come," he said. He
spoke French carefully and clearly, as an educated foreigner
speaks it.

"She did. Do you always call her Madame Clozel?"

[78]

"Yes."

"Why do you?"

"My mother lives in Germany, with my father."

"I see. It would be ungrateful of you not to remain fond of your German mother"—he was aware that the words meant nothing—"and not natural. But you could, perhaps you could remind yourself that another woman actually gave birth to you, and allow her some share in your life."

Looking him in the eyes, the boy said something so atrocious that, if nothing else had done it, it would have given away the enormity of his despair.

"She couldn't help it."

"What do you mean?"

"She couldn't help having me. It happened to her . . . And *she* didn't look after me all these years until now, and give me everything she could think of and show me things and tell me what I should be able to do when I—" he stopped, and forced all expression from his face—"and now I shall never do any of the things we planned—a motorcycle, the university . . ."

"There are universities in France."

"I hate this country," the boy said coldly, "I hate everything to do with it, I hate this house, this village, I hate the way they teach in the school, it's quite stupid. If anyone, if Madame Clozel thinks I shall get used to it, she is mistaken. There is nothing here I don't hate."

"Nothing and no one?" Leighton asked, smiling.

The boy was silent.

"If you like, we can talk German," Leighton said.

"No, thanks."

Vexed by the flicker of contempt in the boy's voice, Leighton said nothing for a moment. He recalled what Aristide Michal had told him about his failure, in the train, to make any sort of contact, even the most elementary, with a young creature so cut off as to be not there. He was not rude, not noisily refractory, not sullen; he was out of reach, by his own will. It was no use talking to him; the words fell back, useless, like pebbles thrown against an iron shutter. And yet, somewhere, he was alive, even terribly alive, and lively, and alert and well-meaning. Leighton felt it, as you feel, in a rock pool, the movement at an immense distance of the open sea.

An emotion he had not known for a longer time than he realized stirred in him, very weakly. It was not pity, not even sympathy for the desperate trapped child facing him with no sign of feeling except a slight twitch of his eyelids.

Perhaps, he thought reluctantly, if I had had a son he would have needed me, a little. I might not have been absolutely alone, dependent on a servant for traces of warmth.

"I should like to be able to help you," he said coolly. "But the truth is I don't know that there is anything I could say to comfort you, or any way you can comfort yourself, since all you want is to get back. To live backwards and wash all this"—he waved a hand—"out of existence. It isn't possible, and so—"

The boy interrupted him, without raising his voice. "And so I have to live here, for years. And nothing—nothing—afterwards —will put it right, or be the same."

My God, he even knows that, Leighton thought.

For the first time, the boy looked as though he might break down and cry. Hurriedly, *to spare himself,* Leighton said,

"Listen. You've seen I'm not trying to comfort you. Perhaps you can believe me when I tell you that there *are* things here, even in St.-Loup-de-Grâce, that you can use for the future, your future. I say use, and I mean: use to be happy."

He stopped, because the boy was not listening. What tenuous link there had been between them, for a moment, had snapped.

"Never mind," he said gently. "But you might remember occasionally that your mother didn't choose to have you in a frightful place, in agony, if you know what that is, and to spend months in the camp you know nothing about, and after that years searching for you. It won't be any help, but it might, I say might, alter the outlook a bit."

Jean Clozel looked at him from eyes so charged with dislike that he felt a momentary irrational fear.

"If she was taken away by force herself, why did she do it to me?"

Why indeed?

"You know where I live," he said. "If you want anything—books, music—I have a decent gramophone—come."

He won't come, he told himself. He held out his hand. The boy took it, and smiled—a smile of such sweetness that Leighton held his breath for a second, in surprise. But he did not say: Thanks, I'll come. He said nothing, but walked in front of Leighton to the door, opened it, stood aside for Leighton to walk through, and shut it at once.

He has gone back to his room, thought Leighton.

He called to his side all his skepticism, his coldness of heart, his refusal, for any reason whatsoever, to pity other people, since it is only and always an excuse for pitying oneself. . . . You are an old fool, he told himself, you have been wasting your time. . . . He could not save himself from the moment of regret, of longing for a warmth so far behind him now that it slipped like a shadow through his icy fingers.

8

The friendship between Jean Clozel, pariah, and the school-master's daughter and only child began less than a week after he came to St.-Loup-de-Grâce. On Saturday afternoon he had walked out alone—of course alone: except during school hours he was avoided as strictly as if he had the plague—to look for the river he knew from the map on the wall of the classroom must be within a mile of the village. It came from the hills to the northwest and entered its first gorge just above the point where the road turned across the long upland pasture belonging, most of it, to old Larrau. This upper gorge was short and not very precipitous: from it, the river emerged on to another stretch of level country and ran, widening but still deep, for some three hundred yards, over a flat stony bottom. As it neared the second of its gorges the current gathered speed until it plunged suddenly, a glacial torrent, and fell four hundred feet between rocky walls into a pool as black as pitch.

From the village there were two ways to reach it. The one Jean Clozel took was the usual and longer, by the road, as far as the monument to the Truchi brothers. He read the inscription with a slight qualm of misgiving. He smiled deliberately, and said aloud,

"What had they done to deserve it, the apes?"

From this point a goat track, turning on itself half a dozen times, and masked by shrubs and stunted oaks, followed the side of the upper gorge and dropped sharply to the lower pasture. As he made his way down it to reach the level stretch of the river, he saw with exasperation that someone, a child, was there already, lying face downward on the bank, dipping one arm in the water. A girl.

Out of defiance, he went on. When he was almost on her, she turned her head toward him, and smiled.

This smile, which narrowed her eyes to very bright slits above her scarlet cheeks, startled him more than if she had spat in his face, which had happened to him several times in the past week.

He knew who she was, and her name—Marthe Vincent. As he still hesitated, she rolled over and sat up in one swift movement, and patted the ground beside her.

"Why don't you sit down?"

He sat down abruptly, his heart, between mistrust, curiosity, and an unwilling reassurance, beating so quickly that he felt sick. After a few minutes, as she went on talking, seeming not to care whether he understood her or not, the fear that he might be going to vomit left him, and he began to catch words and whole phrases, and to attempt phrases of his own. She listened attentively, correcting him, and supplying fresh words.

This first talk was hardly personal at all, though she did tell him about herself that her mother was dead, and her aunt, Agathe, an old stick, not bad, not really a nit, but dull and very pious. She told him that this stretch of the river had a particular name: Black Spring.

Why this name? No one knew. There was no spring, and the water was a cold clear green.

She asked him nothing about himself.

During the last week he had advanced so rapidly in the science of human nature that he could recognize an instinctive tact when he met it.

She succeeded in warning him that if he came here tomorrow afternoon, Sunday, there would be other people. No one ever came here on weekdays. She repeated it: on weekdays it was safe.

"That is why I like it."

"To be alone?" he asked.

"Yes." She narrowed her eyes in the smile he found so strangely reassuring and moving. "But I shall like it if you come."

He repeated stupidly, "If I come."

She laughed. "Yes. Do come."

And on Monday morning she spoke to him during recreation, in front of the others. There were queer looks, but no one accused her. She was Marthe Vincent; her father was not only the schoolmaster but the secretary to the mairie and a friend of the most important men in the neighborhood; a child ill-advised enough to risk offending him could count on worse than sharp words from its parents. Her two intimate friends, one of them the policeman's daughter, the other a granddaughter of Monsieur Paul Larrau, remonstrated with her in secret; she laughed at them, and went on in her serene way, not seeking him out but talking to him whenever their ways crossed.

And—this no one suspected yet—they met at Black Spring not only on Saturday afternoons but, as the days lengthened, two or three times during the week, between the end of school and supper. Marthe had a passion for this stretch of the river which she did not try to explain to him. She saw nothing to explain. The water itself fascinated her. Without thinking about it, she supposed that this boy shared her feeling.

In his own way he did. He could spend a long time without saying a word, watching the movement of the water as it spiraled round stones and between the tough bankside reeds alive with tiny snakes. In the center the current ran strongly, and one of their active amusements was to throw into the calmer water at the side a branch from one of the wind-bitten shrubs growing there, wait for a minute while it drifted toward the center and then race madly along the bank in the hope of being in time to see it swept violently over the lip of the torrent.

Just here, at the lip, a flat rock jutted from the bank into the stream. Except during days when the river was swollen by snow water, the surface of this rock, lifted a few inches out of the water, was dry and a little warm. To lie on it and peer over the edge at the dark column of water plunging down, down, as dense and unyielding as the rocky walls strangling it between their black flanks, gave them an indescribably pleasant feeling of danger and giddiness. "Fabulous," Marthe said, smiling. The rock was not wide enough for the two of them to stretch out on it together. They took it in turn to lie there, dipping a hand in the water to feel the current grip it between icy teeth.

The most dangerous and exciting part of the game was to reach as far out as possible from the end of the rock and try, vainly, to seize a branch or a leaf as it rushed past.

For a good reason, that it was a curiously exhausting excitement, they did not play this rock game very long. The rest of their time, perhaps an hour, on Saturdays as long as two or three hours, they spent racing about the bank, or they sat on the thin harsh grass, talking. At first it had been Marthe who talked, with a few halting interruptions from the boy. Later, she listened more than she talked. All the talk that piled up in him during the day, when he opened his mouth only during class, or outside the school to reply to a jeering remark, or at home to answer his mother as briefly as possible, rushed out now, sometimes with hysterical vehemence.

The day after Leighton had been to see him, he told Marthe about it.

"He came because Madame Clozel asked him to come. He sat there looking like a molting vulture, and talked the way they do at his age—"

"How do you know?"

"What?"

"About old men."

"They think because they're done with everything that nothing is worth a fuss. They don't feel anything—except that they get hungry at the usual times, and their bones ache, and so on—and all they want is not to be disturbed or annoyed by other people, by us, kicking and yelling that things are unfair or beastly. If you're half dead, as they are, what can you possibly know or care about people who are still alive?" He smiled sharply. "I can't help believing that they were always like that, even young. Because I can't imagine myself reaching that state of being half dotty and not caring."

"All the same, if he asked you to go and see him, you could," Marthe said. "He has one whole room crammed with books, a fabulous gramophone, and two pictures my father says are worth a small fortune. I wish I could see them."

"Why can't you?"

"I haven't been invited. You have."

"He doesn't want me to go. He said that because he was bored. He hadn't anything to say to me. Only cant."

Marthe was silent, looking at him with a reflective smile.

"You're very clever," she said. "But in some ways you're not sensible."

"How can I be sensible?" he said violently. "I don't know what's happening at home, and I can't think of anything else, I think about it every night, I tell you, and during the day. Perhaps I'm mad—but suppose you were sent away, to a frightful place where you were expected to be someone else, and there was no one you could ask, nobody who would tell you, what your father was doing, if he was dead, if the house had burned to the ground—nothing—you knew absolutely nothing, and you were absolutely helpless." His voice cracked suddenly. "She may be ill now—and I shan't know."

"You told me—I thought you told me—she promised she would find a way of letting you know if she was very ill, or if they left the farm," Marthe said.

"Yes." He scowled at her. "But how do I know she'll keep her promise?"

"Don't you trust even her?"

He pressed his lips together in the line she knew and was a little afraid of, and after a minute said nearly inaudibly,

"She let them take me."

"What else could she do?" the girl said quietly.

"We could have run away together. I—I begged her."

"You would have been caught."

"I daresay. But they might not have taken me from her, the beasts. I hate them, I hate everyone here—"

"Except me," she interrupted, smiling at him.

"Yes, of course except you," he said impatiently. "But the others, and this ugly horrible country. And I shall be here for years—every day is another day gone, another wasted day, years and years of life wasted, as uselessly wasted as if I was in prison. That's what you don't understand!"

"I understand that you hate it. But, Jean, this is where you live! If you don't live *here,* in the village, you're not living any-where, you might as well be Monsieur Leighton, too old to feel."

He said sarcastically,

"You're very clever today."

"No. Sensible. There are dozens of things I'd like, I'd like a bicycle, and mamma to be alive, and most of all I'd like Aunt Agathe to take her long face and sermons somewhere else. But every minute I spend thinking about her is an absolute waste."

"You're talking rubbish," he said, through clenched teeth.

But his fits of half-incoherent rage did not frighten her. "Well, if I am," she said lightly, "there must be some way you could be a little happier here, however much you loathe the place and the people."

"Yes, yes, I know! If you can't have what you like, like what you have . . . I can't bear that tripe, I can't bear people who take any sort of tenth-rate dull life they can get and say thank

[87]

you for it. I know what I want and what I had, and no one, not even you, is going to make me say I enjoy this place, or forgive the brutes who made me come here. One day I'll punish them for it, I'll—" He choked: he had turned pale and his eyes started at her.

"Jean," she said quickly, drawing back.

He dropped his head. "I'm sorry."

"Never mind." She looked at him with her wide ravishing smile. "There's one little thing you could do, you know, that would make your life a bit easier. You could wear different clothes."

"These are my ordinary clothes, I wore them all the time at home. What's wrong with them?"

"Don't pretend you don't know what's wrong with them. They're far too good for everyday."

"I haven't any others."

"Your mother would get you some like everyone else's."

"My—" he closed his lips tightly.

"She *is* your mother."

"I dress as I like to," he said coldly, "and I certainly shall not ask Madame Clozel to get me anything."

"Oh, all right. . . . I shall have to go soon. Do you want to tell me about the farm now?"

This, too, was a game they played, except that for Jean Clozel it was less game than rite. They had begun it the afternoon Marthe said,

"Suppose I was blind, and you were taking me to see where you lived—I mean before you came here. What would you say? You'd say something like: Mind the steps now. Or: Over there on the left is the pigeon loft, you can hear the noise they make— and so on. . . . Pretend you're guiding me and tell me about it."

Reluctantly at first, then with growing energy and pleasure, he took her about the farm and country surrounding it, describing the scenes and objects that, being blind, she couldn't see for herself. They opened the wide double gate, and he made her stand still to smell the limes and listen—it was, he said, June—to the sound the bees made moving in and out of the leaves. From here there were two ways they could go into the house itself—through the yard, with its barns and sheds, into the long brick-floored passage with the dairy on the right and the door into the kitchen on the left: or they could go round in front along the graveled path between the flower beds, and stand a few minutes looking across them to the nearest of the fields, with the stream and the immense plane trees—"everywhere green, so many colors, so fresh, not like this dry hard place"—before he opened the white-painted door with its heavy brass handle and stepped inside the cool hall smelling of soap and dried woodruff, and so into the living room or up the well-polished stairs into the bedrooms, and above them the wide attics . . .

Today he decided to take her round his "mother's" bedroom. He told her where the chests stood in the room, and what they contained, opened cupboards, and made her finger the linen sheets on the bed and the huge soft down-filled quilt. Suddenly —they were crossing the room from the window to the other side, and there were chairs in the way—he stopped.

"Go on," Marthe said.

"Wait—be careful—there is this chair with the curved back and no arms, and the other, the armchair, has an embroidered cushion, yellow and—and—I can't remember."

He got to his feet, and said again,

"I can't remember."

"It doesn't matter," Marthe said calmly.

"I—you—" Now his eyes had become stones in his head, and he thrust his head forward as though he wanted to strike with it. Controlling his voice, he said, "Go on home."

"Aren't you coming?"

Usually they walked together as far as the foot of the goat path, then Marthe went on ahead and he hung about for a quarter of an hour before following her, so that they ran no risk of being seen together on the road into the village. They never spoke about this precaution; they had taken it instinctively, from a shared silent recognition that adults are not to be trusted.

"No. Not yet."

"Very well."

Watching him from the corner of her eyes, she went through the form of brushing fragments of grass from her skirt, and when he took no notice, and said nothing, she turned and walked away quickly, without looking back.

Is she vexed? he wondered. At the moment, he did not care whether she were or not. Her little figure dwindled into the distance, and he forgot about her. His head was filled by a swirling vapor, like the dark spirals of water below the surface of the stream. It confused him, he took a step forward, then another, without reflecting, and after a time found he had got as far as the start of the goat path. Instead of taking it, he turned off to the left along a path even narrower and more stony, leading directly across the flank of the hill on which St.-Loup clung like a wasp's nest. This was the other way to reach Black Spring from the village, and no one in his senses took it. There were places where the path was less than a foot wide, hung between the wall of gray calcined rock and the precipice, a drop of four or five hundred feet to fetch up in a ravine bristling with livid pointed rocks, and in few places was it easy walking.

He had not a particularly good head for heights, and after coming this way once, out of curiosity, he had sworn to himself that he would never try it again. He moved along it now like a sleepwalker, placing his feet without looking at the ground, his eyes on the opposite hillside and its labyrinth of rocks and few gnarled trees jutting from an invisible ledge. It was when he was crossing one of the worst places that he came to himself, and stopped, with a sickening throb of fear at the center of his body. He went on slowly. There was no turning back.

Trying involuntarily to contract his body so that it would take up less room on the path, he looked only at the ground under his feet. The confusion in his mind cleared up, leaving it empty of all but a cold anger. It was not anger against a particular person or persons, it was a state, a hard round shape like a marble between and behind his eyes.

He reached the last easier slope and scrambled up it hurriedly. This path led straight into the lower village through an alleyway between two houses, and came out almost opposite the house he never allowed himself to think of except as Madame Clozel's.

When he went in, she was laying the table in the kitchen for their evening meal. He was going up the stairs to his room when she spoke.

"Have you been for a walk?"

"Yes."

"I think it's warmer—almost spring."

He did not answer, and she said, "Don't stay in your room, Jeannot, supper is ready now."

Frowning, he turned back, and took his seat at the narrow table with its red and white cloth and the thick white plates and bowls, into which she ladled the soup. It was good soup, made of vegetables and potatoes, with olive oil. At first he had disliked the taste of the olive oil she poured into the soup and had asked her not to put any in his. Lately, without speaking about it, he had taken to helping himself from the decanter with its narrow neck like a fowl's.

"Why do you frown?" she asked him, with a faint smile.

He hesitated, and decided to answer truthfully. "I don't like being called Jeannot."

"Why not?"

"It's a stupid name."

"It was what your father liked me to call him."

He shrugged his shoulders. He could reply either: My father is still living in a farm near Frankfurt. Or: My real name is Joachim. Both sentences trembled on the end of his tongue. He rejected them and did not speak.

"Did you walk far?"

"No."

She seemed to make an effort to ask her next question. "I've been wondering—do you get on well at school, with the other boys?"

"Yes."

"Do you like any of them?"

"Not particularly."

"Don't you like any of the children?"

"They're all right."

"It's not an easy village to get to know the people," she said. "You know, I was born here, I lived here until I married your father and went to Paris to live. But I don't think there is anyone alive now that I think of as my friend. Except, yes, Monsieur Michal. But he is everybody's friend."

Something stirred at the bottom of his mind that was neither curiosity nor politeness, and almost without meaning to do it he asked a question, a thing he never did unless it were strictly necessary, something he had to know only to be able to find his way round in this purgatory.

"Why didn't you go back to Paris after . . . ?"

"After the camp, do you mean? I really don't know. I suppose—it's an instinct, when you've been all but destroyed, to come home. . . . My mother and father, your grandparents, were dead—but I didn't know that until I got here—and there were several people I had always known and who knew me."

He was silent, and after a moment she said, calmly, lightly,

"Some of them, too, would rather I had died in that camp."

The words reached him across a distance. Instinctively, he shut his ears to them. If she thinks she can get at me by talking about that place, he said to himself. A glint of the anger lying about in his brain focused itself on her; he sat rigid, feeling in his muscles the impulse to smash crockery and throw himself, howling, at the walls of the neat stiflingly small room.

"How long is it since you came?" she asked suddenly.

He looked at her without speaking.

[92]

"Never mind," she said, with her small smile. "I know how long it is. And you don't like it any better, you don't like this house, nor the village, nor"—she hesitated briefly—"me. But you know—no, you don't, but you will—in time you'll get more used to us. If I didn't believe that . . . But you will. By the force of things—"

He interrupted in a voice as colorless as his face at this moment, dry, impersonal.

"Things don't force anyone." Anyone who doesn't choose to be forced, he added silently.

"Oh. If you think about it, you'll see that in the end they have more force than anything men and women do, or have, more than pride or love or—"

"No."

He got up, pushing aside his plate and the empty soup bowl, and went upstairs to his room.

For a long time that night he lay in his bed with eyes open, tearing at his brain to drag from it the shapes and colors of the things in his foster mother's bedroom. Not only one cushion, but other familiar objects, so familiar that perhaps he had never consciously looked at them, had become drab and formless; and the more feverishly he pursued them through the thin fog behind his eyes the less substantial they became, shadows in a dissolving world of shadows. . . . His anger turned against himself; the veins in his wrists and long childishly thin neck throbbed until he thought they were breaking open, and suddenly he began crying and had to turn on his face to stifle the sounds in his pillow.

You, he said to himself, you swine, you mean dirty disloyal swine, you're letting her down—after all you said.

When he had no more tears in him, he fell asleep. He dreamed himself into the kitchen at the farm; it was early evening, neither light nor dark, and deliciously warm. His German mother was sitting at the long table busied with something indistinct, her fine large gentle hands, with the two gold rings, moving deftly among a collection of jars. Thankful in body and mind to be back with her again, he watched eagerly. For a time his happiness was so acute it was almost tangible, another presence in the room. Then a vague feeling of uncertainty seeped into it. A suspicion that this was not going to last, he was not really safe. And now the room was becoming spectral and darker, and her figure at the table dwindled, fading. Straining his eyes, he cried out, begging her not to let him go, to keep him with her. Then it was not she who was leaving him, but he himself who was forced to go away. Desperate, he told her over and over again: It's you I love, not the other one, oh, not the other one; I'll come back tomorrow night, wait here for me, I'll come back, I promise.

He woke in the whitewashed room, in the little iron bed, alone. You could not say that, at his age, he was without hope. But he felt that he was alone.

9

On one or two evenings a week during the slack months, Philippe went off on the Vespa as early as eight o'clock, to amuse himself somewhere, almost always in a dance hall. This evening he went off to Nice. At midnight, when Michal and Lotte went to bed, he had not come back. This was usual. It was not usual for him to be still out at five, when Michal went down to the kitchen to make the coffee.

Putting his head into the boy's room to tell him that he was going to drive into Nice now, he was mildly surprised by the empty bed. Philippe did now and then stay the night in Nice, with a young fellow from the village who had moved there to work, but on these occasions, because Lotte fretted about the risk of an accident on the tricky road, he always telephoned to let them know.

Taking her coffee to Lotte, he told her,

"The boy didn't come home."

She sat up quickly, running a hand through her weight of black gleaming hair. "What?"

"Some young woman," Michal said, "and they both fell much too soundly asleep."

"Nonsense. I don't believe it," she said violently.

Her violence startled him. So did the agitation that had seized her: the hand holding her cup shook and spilled coffee over the sheet, and she put it down and got out of bed and began to dress, pulling on chemise and stockings in furious jerky haste.

"What's the matter with you?" asked Michal, smiling. "The boy's a normal boy."

"No," she said, "there's been an accident. That Vespa. I knew it would happen. I'm coming with you to Nice."

He tried to laugh her out of it, and was startled afresh by the rage with which she turned on him. When he brought the car out of the shed to the front of the hotel she was waiting there to get in, and sat beside him in silence as he drove, a little more carefully than usual, past the shuttered houses to the upper square, and out of it on to the road.

"Is this the way he usually comes from Nice?" she asked. "Or would he take the way round?"

"How do I know?" said Michal. "Almost certainly he comes this way, it's so much shorter." He added dryly, "You know, my dear, no young man—Philippe is twenty—cares to have his parents running in search of him when he doesn't come home at the usual time. He has two arms, two legs and the rest of it. Let him alone to use them."

The effort she made to control herself was obvious in her voice. "I daresay. But I know—I say I know that's not the reason. There's some other reason. I'm certain he's had an accident. I've been expecting it ever since he bought the Vespa."

The whole way until they reached the coast road, she sat stiffly upright, turning her head from side to side, sometimes leaning far out to be able to see ahead. The light, still gray and cool when they left the village, strengthened by leaps and bounds, and they drove into Nice, for part of the way along the

front, past a smoothly naked morning sea. It was not yet eight
o'clock. She wanted Michal to take her directly to the house in
one of the dark narrow odorous streets behind the market where
Philippe's friend had his one room. He refused.

"If you must make a nuisance of yourself to the boy," he told
her good-humoredly, "and embarrass him, I'd as soon not be
present. Come back here, to the Âne Noir, I'll wait for you
until nine, after that you must get yourself home."

She was back in less than half an hour, before he had finished
in the market; her face was composed, but she looked in some
way older than usual. He caught himself thinking: She's beginning to look her age. . . . He felt a light grief.

"Well?" he said gently.

"He wasn't there." She hesitated, and said in a rough voice,
"What's more, he hasn't slept there for weeks now—months."

"Well, that's not—"

She interrupted him. "You know perfectly well that a dozen
times this year he has—so he told us—stayed the night with
Ricou. It wasn't true."

Michal shrugged. "What did I tell you? Come, Lotte, you're
behaving like—" He had been going to say: like an old woman.
He changed it to—"like an idiot. What do you expect?"

"I expect the truth," she said harshly.

Do all women resent it so much? he wondered. "We shall
find him at home. And I tell you, I shall be annoyed if you
make any kind of fuss. If at his age he isn't allowed a few lies
to keep his life to himself . . ."

"But why Philippe?" she said in the same unpleasant voice.

"Why not?"

On the drive home, she did not open her mouth, and as
soon as they reached the hotel went straight to Philippe's room.

There was no need for her to tell Michal that he was not in
it. He knew it already, because, when he drove the car into the
shed, the Vespa was still not there.

By now, he himself was a little puzzled. He could think of

[97]

reasons why Philippe had not come home—he might have changed his mind and gone as far as Marseilles, and overslept there—but what really was surprising was that he, usually so careful not to upset Lotte, had not telephoned to let them know he was all right. It was not like him.

To Lotte he said easily that there was some simple explanation, some excuse, and whatever it was she must accept it calmly. "You can't treat him as if he were a girl." In his own mind he decided to tell Philippe sharply that what he did and where he went was entirely his own business, but he must take care in future not to alarm his mother by going off on his murderous Vespa for a few hours and staying away more than half a day.

As he formed the phrases in his mind, a thought—one he had not had for years—struck him: She's not his mother, nor am I his father . . . He pushed it angrily aside.

By twelve o'clock Lotte's anxiety had become uncontrollable. Standing in front of Michal in their room, her fine dark eyes stupid with fear, mouth trembling, she said,

"Either you ring the police, or I will."

Since there was no other way to calm her, he rang up the police station in Grasse and asked to speak to the Commissioner. The sound of Gaudo's abrupt powerful voice convinced him that he was making a fool of himself and of Philippe, but he told his story, adding,

"It's certainly nothing at all, nothing wrong, the boy is probably on his way home at this moment or still asleep after playing the goat until breakfast, but—you know how it is—my wife is convinced he's lying at the foot of a cliff, with the Vespa piled on top of him, or in hospital after a quarrel with a bus. If you—"

Gaudo's harsh chuckling laugh cut him short. "Leave it to me. You're right, of course, he's asleep—sleeping it off. I'll wake him up. Tell Madame Michal that from me."

There were only four people for lunch. Lotte had shut herself in the bedroom, and with young Truchi's help Michal saw to them without her. Had the restaurant been full, he would not have allowed her to behave in this grotesque way, he was a reasonable man, he could indulge her in a mood, but he was not a fool. Since he could do without her easily, he let her alone. And the truth was, he had begun to be uneasy himself— merely because this was the first time Philippe had behaved irresponsibly.

At five o'clock he was standing in the doorway of the hotel, looking along the street, when the nose of the black police car came into sight at the top of the steep drop from the square. The current of fear in his body paralyzed him for a moment. Lotte was right, there had been an accident.

As the car drew up at the hotel, he saw that Gaudo was not alone in it. Beside the driver there was another person, a woman, a young woman.

He forced himself to move, to open the car door.

Stepping out, Gaudo said harshly over his shoulder, "Stay where you are." He turned to Michal and said more quietly, "All right, Michal. No accident, he's not dead, not hurt. I'll tell you the rest inside."

Except for "old nanny goat" and two men standing up to the bar, the café was empty. Michal opened the door of the bedroom, and looked inside. Lotte was lying across the bed, face downward. She swung herself round, and sat up, her dress rucked halfway up her thigh. Catching sight of Gaudo's broad body behind Michal's shoulder, she pressed her hand over her mouth, eyes dilated like a madwoman's.

Michal came in, drawing Gaudo in with him, and closed the door.

"It's all right," he said, "the boy is all right."

He smoothed her skirt over her knees, and touched her face: it was hot and moist. She pushed his hand away.

"Well?" She looked at Gaudo. "What is happening? Where is he?"

Before he answered, Gaudo settled himself in the only comfortable chair in the room, leaning back in it and stretching his long fat legs. He spoke without any haste, keeping his eyes on Lotte, in what was for him a genial voice.

"What is happening I don't know—yet. Where he is I can tell you, but you must listen to me quietly, eh? You'll be surprised. He's in Paris. Well, I suppose he's in Paris. He left on the express last night and he had a ticket to Paris in his pocket. He put his Vespa in the yard, and it would have taken us a little longer to find out, but the old fellow in charge knows him by sight—he has left the Vespa there several times. He dropped a scarf, and the old chap ran after him with it as far as the ticket office and gave it to him and got a tip. The clerk, of course, doesn't know him, but he remembered the face when my boys described it. After all, it's a face, eh? Not one of those you don't notice when you look at it."

He might have been talking to give the other two time to take in what had happened. When he stopped, it was still Lotte he watched. She had not moved, and did not move now, sitting on the edge of the bed like a statue in dark clay of a Roman matron.

Glancing at her, Michal noticed that her nostrils were drawn together, pinched, as though she were trying not to breathe, or could breathe only with pain. His own only sensation was bewilderment. He said,

"But—what's this about? Why should he go to Paris? Why Paris?"

The look on Gaudo's heavy sagging face was for an instant one of pity. Then he said coolly,

"Perhaps your wife has an idea?"

"No," Lotte said. Her broad eyelids flickered. "No."

"How the devil could she have any idea?" Michal said. He had a spasm of anger, against the fog he was groping in, and against Gaudo. He suspected the policeman of—but, no, he did not know what he suspected. He had a feeling that he was being deliberately tormented; it bewildered and exasperated him. "What's going on?"

There was a brief pause. Gaudo sat up, splaying out his knees, and setting his hands on them, like an old woman preparing herself for a comfortable chat. He spoke very soberly.

"Listen, my friend. You're not going to like this. The truth is —for the last month, since the robbery, I've been watching Master Philippe closely. That means—more closely, much more closely, than at any time. I can't really say I had my eye on him before this, but I know a few things about him which you certainly don't; you don't know the sort of friends he has in Nice and Marseilles, young good-looking impudent *scum,* the little friends of grotesquely rich old women, American or English— ours are usually more discreet in their ridiculous excitements. As you can imagine, none of them had the successes Philippe has had. He had only to look at one of these old or not so old poor randy creatures with those eyes of his, y'know, *stroking* them, and they fell on their knees imploring him to take all they had."

He broke off, with a little whinny of mirth, and said to Lotte,

"Eh, Madame Michal? Even you, even as his mother, you must have noticed what he could do with that face of his."

She did not speak. Michal said violently—the violence was some slight relief for the feeling of suffocation in the upper half of his body,

"If all this is true, why didn't you warn us?"

Gaudo moved his shoulders clumsily. "Why should I interfere, and get the boy into trouble—so long as all he was doing was relieve a few silly women of their money and their itch? . . . It's only in this last month I began thinking that his, let's say his amusements, weren't perfectly harmless."

"Well, go on," Michal said, "go on, go on."

"Have you missed any money—I'm not talking about the robbery."

"No."

"Quite sure?"

"Good God, man, do you think I don't know to a penny what I have?"

"All right, all right." He turned his head to stare at Lotte. "How much did you give him yesterday?"

"I?" She half closed her eyes. "Nothing. Why should I?"

"Over the last year—or two years—how much have you given him?"

This time, she looked at him with a gleam of anger. "Nothing."

"Madame Michal," he said, bringing out for the first time one of his organ notes, "you want the boy found, I take it, you want the truth—whatever it is. The only way I can help you— believe me, I want to help you—is by knowing all you can tell me about his, h'm, habits. Don't tell me you haven't been giving him money to spend in Nice and the rest—I know better. Tell me something—didn't it ever occur to you to wonder why he hadn't enough with what your husband gave him for the sort of places he told you he went to? You've been very simple, eh?"

This stung her. She stood up, red in the face. "If you know so much, why ask me?"

"Sit down, please," Gaudo said dryly. "Please keep calm, I'm not trying to vex you, all I want to do is to help you."

A cold sense of unreality seized Michal. "Have you been giving him money?" he asked her.

She did not look at him. "Yes. When I had it to spare."

"Ah," Gaudo said, smiling, "how much did you hand over yesterday?"

She hesitated. "Five thousand francs."

"God damn it—"

Michal's exclamation did not startle her. She said hardily, "It was what you gave me."

"Not to be used for—"

"Be good enough not to lose your temper, my dear friend,"

[102]

Gaudo said easily. "I have a few more questions. If you like, I will ask you both to come with me, and make it a formal affair, you needn't talk to me now, it's just as you please, if you would rather not have a friendly conversation. But you asked me to find the boy, and I came here to tell you everything I know. It's up to you."

"What do you want me to tell you?" Lotte said.

Gaudo leaned forward. "At the time of the robbery, you told us that Philippe did not come upstairs all evening, he didn't set eyes on the two young fellows who wanted to stay the night?"

"No, he never saw them."

"Not even after dinner, when they were in the café?"

"No."

"Wasn't that a little strange? With your husband away, you didn't think of speaking to him when two men you didn't know asked you for a room?"

"Why should I?"

"Well, perhaps not. After all, you're not a young woman. . . . And now, just tell me. You said that it was only that afternoon, Saturday afternoon, that you told him there was all this money in the safe."

"Yes."

"Philippe himself said that you told him on Tuesday."

Something that might have been a smile crossed Lotte's wide mouth, drawing it down at one end. She looked directly into Gaudo's small dangerous eyes.

"What are you trying to say now?" she asked in an almost lazy voice, deep and on its own level as sonorous as his. "That Philippe helped them to take the money? That he had time to make plans?"

"Did you tell him on the Tuesday?"

"No. On Saturday."

"Why are you protecting him? That he knew the money was there doesn't mean he arranged for two of his friends to come and get it."

What seemed a knot of black swollen veins rose behind Michal's eyes, stupefying him again. He began a sentence which Gaudo cut short by a scythe-like movement of his arm.

"Wait. Wait a minute. You are sure, eh?, you are quite sure that you kept to yourself, until that very afternoon, that your husband had left all this money and the keys of the safe with you? Please think very carefully. You may be very sorry if you are forgetting to tell us something."

"Whatever Philippe has done," Lotte said coldly, "he is not a scoundrel, he had no hand in robbing two people who have— who have done everything in the world for him."

"Two people, eh?"

"I've had enough of this," Michal said, without raising his voice. "Anything else you want to know, ask in some other place, at some other time."

Before answering, Gaudo got himself out of the awkwardly low chair.

"I tell you, my friends," he said affably, his large face so astute, so arrantly the provincial Machiavelli, that it had its own innocence, "I am only your friend now, not some other person, not a policeman. All I want—apart from bringing two or more rascals to their proper end—is to spare you as much as you can be spared. Perhaps that won't be much, but all the same . . . That's why I have fetched a young woman here from Nice to tell you something in all decency rather than let it drop on your heads. I have no reason, I may say, to do this for you, I do it out of pure friendship. Excuse me."

He opened the door, and finding the café empty except for "old nanny goat," took a few steps through it, and bellowed,

"You. Martin. Bring her here."

The young woman who came into the bedroom, pushed forward by the constable's hand on her narrow shoulder, could not be more than seventeen or eighteen, thin in face and immature in body, but with brutally defined good looks, large eyes of a waspish brilliance between two thick swatches of blond hair, a slender nose, and grossly overpainted lips parted to show the edge of small teeth. Looking round her with comic insolence, she gave Lotte an appraising stare, and smiled, not an unfriendly smile, but not of her age.

Without thinking, Michal pushed forward a chair, and she sat down, crossing her legs and fluttering at him lashes like small quills.

"What," Gaudo said, "do you know about Philippe Michal? No, wait, I'll tell them myself. And if Monsieur or Madame Michal has anything to ask you, you can do yourself nothing but good by answering them. *I* say so."

He is enjoying himself, Michal thought with helpless rage.

"The name of this young woman is Rouché, Lili Rouché. She is the only one, perhaps, of his girl friends who has never turned on him, however casually he treated her. The others were not so patient, eh, Rouché?"

The girl spoke in a thin hoarse voice, like a child with a chest cold. "He could make you do anything when he felt, y'know, loving. Other times he could be a devil. But there was no one like him."

Because Gaudo was looking at Lotte, Michal glanced at her. Her face was hard and sullen. She would like to get hold of the creature and beat her mercilessly, he thought. Her hands were trembling a little.

"Let's get on," Gaudo said amiably. "This week, three days ago, in fact, the greedy boy helps himself to all the money poor Rouché has saved during the past year, not a great sum, but worth slipping from under the mattress where she keeps it, and he knows she keeps it. Well—she has been waiting for him to turn up again, to accuse him and make him hand it back. Instead, it is the police who turn up this afternoon and tell her he has bolted. Naturally, she loses her temper, and tells them everything she knows about him. Everything. That's correct, Rouché, eh?"

"Correct enough," the girl answered. "You might add that

I've no objection to him taking their bits and pieces off the old sows who pick him up when he smiles at them, but when it comes to skinning your friends, it's—" she looked from the corners of her fiercely blue eyes at Lotte—"in present company I won't say what it is."

Lotte stood up, her body rigid with the loathing she ran easily into her voice. "You have a fine idea of us, Monsieur Gaudo, to bring this creature, this little whore, into our room to empty her slops. Why you should believe her story is your business, but to bring her here—"

The girl cut her short in the same childish voice. "Are you calling me a liar, you?"

Lotte did not glance at her. "Have the goodness to take her away," she said to Gaudo.

Jumping up quickly, all at once, like a young dog, the girl said, chanted rather,

"Let me tell you something. You think I didn't know him, your Philippe? Well, I knew him extra-or-din-arily well, he told me everything, I tell you, everything about you, he told me you have a large mole— here—" she pressed a nicotine-stained finger with a long nail between her scarcely noticeable breasts—"and it gives him goose flesh to look at it, and—"

She stopped, because the other woman had dropped back on to the bed, and was swaying, her face drawn and discolored, as though she were about to faint. Moving quickly, Michal took hold of her, but she sat up, pushing him off, and spoke to Gaudo.

"I don't know what you thought you were doing. But you must be a fool if you suppose that I shall now begin to tell lies about Philippe—" her eyes started at him—"I told you and I tell you again: he knew nothing about the money being here until a couple of hours or so before the men who took it turned up. Shout, talk yourself black in the face, you can't get past that. . . . If he hadn't been innocent, do you think he would have told you that he had known about it since Tuesday? He got it wrong—it was Saturday—but if he hadn't been innocent he'd have taken good care, wouldn't he, to guard himself? Think that one out, Monsieur Gaudo."

"Unless," Gaudo said softly, "he expected you to say Tuesday and thought he had better tell the same story."

"Go away," she said, lowering her voice, "and take your—"

Rolling his eyes at her, Gaudo said, "Hush, hush, my good woman." He jerked his head at the girl. "Off you go, Rouché—and sit quietly in the car, like a good child, no leaning out, and wait for me. I shan't be a minute."

He watched her walk out, moving her legs like a marionette in a skirt so narrow that at each tiny step it slid far above her knee.

"I want a photograph of Philippe," he said, as the door shut.

"Why?" Michal asked.

"Why d'you think? To keep under my pillow? We're going to circulate it through the country, railway station posts, harbor police, airfield police, any night club and café in Paris where young fellows of his sort feel at home." He smiled pityingly. "With that face I give him a week, say, two weeks unless he lives like a nun, which isn't likely."

It cost Michal a drop or two of blood to hand over the small amateur snapshot which was the only photograph taken of Philippe in the past five years: it had been taken in profile, and for all its inadequacy it brought out the delicacy, the hovering indelible charm, of his good looks. Easing it out of its cardboard mount, he thought dully: It's not true. Impossible.

Gaudo pushed it in his pocket and went off. As he shook hands with him he gave Michal an almost affectionate glance from his savage little eyes. Lotte had turned her back, and he ignored her.

Alone with her, Michal looked at her for a minute in silence. His strongest feeling was still one of bewilderment, a gray suffocating fog shot through by flashes of pure rage. Trying to rid himself of the fog, he stretched his thick neck forward, moving his head on it.

"Why did you give Philippe money?" he asked.

She did not answer.

"Why didn't you tell me he was spending more money than he had? I didn't keep him short."

Without looking at him, she said,

"I wanted to give him things."

This moved him strangely. But he was more moved by the ugliness of her face at this moment, drawn out by the grooves leading down from the sides of her nose, the long mouth stretched in a line of unspeakable bitterness: even her eyes seemed to be retreating to the back of her head.

"My poor girl," he said heavily, "this is a bad business. But you're not to blame."

Again she did not answer, and he laid his hand on her shoulder in a brief caress. She shook it off with surprising violence.

"Leave me alone," she said sharply. She lifted her head and looked round the room, her upper lip rolled under, in a mockery of a smile. "Isn't there anywhere in this house I can be alone?"

He turned and left her. In the café, "old nanny goat" took one look at his face, and poured him out a cognac. He drank it, forgetting to speak, and went down to the kitchen, to cook, this evening, with his venomous anger and uncertainty.

10

With whatever tools it had been prepared, George Leighton ate his dinner with a more obvious enjoyment than usual, now and again lifting his head to send round the room a glance from an eye which some thought, some repressed excitement, was making phosphorescent, like an animal's in the dark.

At the end of the meal, when Michal brought him his coffee, he said,

"This evening I don't feel like sitting upstairs. Perhaps you would do me the great kindness of sitting down here with me, for a time, if they can do without you in the café. Have you any left of the 1911 armagnac?"

"Two bottles."

"I should like one."

Before bringing it, Michal went upstairs to the café. Of the circle, only Pibourdin was here. At the sight of Michal he allowed a smile of virile sweetness to spread across his plump face, a face Paul Larrau compared to a baby's bottom. Michal thought savagely: Like the rest of them he has by now heard as much as the police know and a great deal more. He felt certain that neither the doctor nor Blaise Vincent would turn up this evening. Looking past Pibourdin, he spoke to "old nanny goat" and told her she would have to stay late, he had work to do in the restaurant. The Arab was in his usual corner, his thin dark hands folded round his café-filtre: on an impulse he ordered her to take the man another, on the house.

When he brought the armagnac to Leighton's table, he set down with it two glasses, and said without a smile,

"The condition of my opening this bottle is that I do not charge you for it, and that we drink level. Is it agreed?"

"If you like," Leighton said, displeased.

Ignoring his tone, Michal poured the armagnac carefully, sat down, tasted it, and said,

"You know what's happened, of course."

Leighton jerked his head up. "What? What's happened. You know I know nothing unless I'm told it here. No one in the village would tell Ahmed that a war had broken out."

He listened attentively while Michal, as briefly and flatly as possible, told him the whole story, even about the young woman. One sunken vulturine eye watched the play of feeling on Michal's hard and sunburned face, noting that his habit of stroking the great mustache curled across it had become a nervous trick. At the end he said in a voice of the greatest simplicity,

"Now and then I've regretted having no son, but I've been spared a great deal of unnecessary anguish. Absurdly unnecessary—since the most elementary reasoning in the world should remind a parent to expect nothing from a child after the age of puberty. At that age they should be cut off—emotionally speaking."

"That's true," Michal said. He added roughly, "The ridiculous thing is that, even now, I have to remind myself that he isn't my son. I've grafted him on myself too successfully."

More fool you, thought Leighton. "I've never taken into my house either a child or an animal. An arid life, some would say.

I say: tranquil, sensible. Children bore me—I detest immature minds. What's more, I'm incapable of sacrificing myself for any human being, of any age. Or sex. I can't imagine circumstances in which I'd deprive myself willingly of a single pleasure, a single satisfaction. This life is all we have, a unique chance."

"Did you plan your life like that?"

"From a certain age, yes."

"Ah, well," Michal said, "the rest of us don't plan our lives, we make plans. A different affair altogether. What happens to us is that every step leads to the next and the next, until we arrive where we hadn't the remotest idea of going. You've been fortunate."

Still eying him with a heartless curiosity, Leighton said, "Your wife, I suppose, is very distressed."

"She's partly responsible. She ought to have told me he was throwing money about."

"Are you sure you know everything now?"

"What do you mean?"

Leighton dipped his great nose toward his glass. "I've always found it as hard to get the whole truth out of a woman as picking a lobster's claws. They're tortuous by instinct."

The anger wrenching Aristide Michal's body was wholly undirected, nothing more than the sharp edge of his sense of uncertainty and demoralization.

"We're only at the beginning," he said under his breath. "Tomorrow we go into Grasse to be questioned or make a statement or what the hell you call it. I thought—talking to Gaudo—we'd finished with that."

Leighton spoke sharply. "You can insist on your lawyer being there. You should. Don't trust yourself to the police—especially when they tell you they're being friendly. The friendship of a Gaudo . . . ! Get yourself a lawyer."

"Jouassaint? That born Jesuit? No, thanks."

"You're unwise."

"Perhaps."

"The police—the police in this country especially—will use any means, from bullying to simple exhaustion, to trap you or your wife into a humiliating position."

The mocking line at the end of Michal's hard stubborn mouth deepened. He said lightly,

"What makes you think I can be worse humiliated than I am already? . . . Let me tell you something I've discovered—*There are no more families.*"

He got up to make out his bill for the only remaining customer. When he returned to the table, he saw in Leighton's eyes the same malicious excitement he had noticed earlier in the evening. Something has happened to him, too, he thought coldly. What the devil can happen to a man who has never in his life laid himself open?

Refilling the glasses, he asked,

"What are we celebrating?"

"Ah," Leighton said. The mischievousness of a very old infant flushed his shrunken face. "The concluding sentence of my book."

"Finished? Good."

"Have you never wanted to know what I was writing about?"

"Since you're not a writer, I always supposed it was about yourself."

"You were partly right. Half right." He paused. The color left his cheeks, but those predatory eyes were full of a disquieting gaiety. "I should like to tell you the gist of it."

"We have more than half the bottle," said Michal, touching it.

"Good, good. It should be enough. . . . How old d'you think I am?"

"Seventy?" Michal said. He had knocked off ten years.

"Seventy-six. In 1920, when I came out of the Army of Occupation, I was forty. My first day in London out of uniform I walked past a shop in—oh never mind where, the street means nothing to you—and remembered that I needed handkerchiefs. The petty silliness of these accidents that decide our lives. It was a large store, not the kind of shop I should have gone into if I'd been in a less euphoric state of mind. I went in by a door that took me through the part of the shop where they sold women's stockings and such, there was some discreet excitement going on—the store detective had just picked up a girl, the pockets of her coat crammed with oddments she'd stolen, and was taking her off somewhere. I have never seen a more ravishingly beautiful young female in my life, not only beautiful—seductive, irresistible, anything you like that describes quite exceptional looks. I was . . . let's say, moved, troubled."

For less than a second his railing arrogant voice deepened almost to tenderness.

"Yes, troubled, my friend. . . . I went to some pains to follow the affair, I saw her tried, and given a month in a woman's prison —it was her second attempt at shoplifting—and when she was discharged I met her outside the prison . . . Not to bore you with too many details of my attack of lunacy—six weeks later I married her. She was twenty, half my age, not a virgin, but in some way, some disturbing equivocal way, fresher than if she had been. You can't conceive that. She hadn't been on the streets, but no doubt in another year . . . She was wholly sensual, and wholly charming and untouched—yes, untouched. And—this surprised me in a young woman of her class—I discovered that she was intelligent and quick-witted, she knew it wasn't going to be easy for her to step out of nowhere into the world I lived in then, and she begged me to teach her. It was to please her— after we had agreed on marriage—that I invented an interesting background of illegitimacy and engaged an elderly woman who was supposed to have taken her from the hands of her aristocratic father and brought her up in complete seclusion." He laughed— a crackling derisive noise. "You see why cheap romances are so popular—they follow the natural slant of our kinds. . . . This woman was still alive fifteen years ago, and able to sign a statement I had drawn up for her by my lawyers."

He laughed again.

"I hope you'll believe me if I say that there is nothing abnormal about me, I'm not defective, sexually, none of the women I lived with before I met her had any cause for complaint. For some reason, inexplicable to me now, I didn't touch her before our marriage. Then I failed with her—a total fiasco. The first night. She was very kind about it, very charming and tactful—and she refused to let me come near her again. Let's be the closest friends in the world, she said seriously—smiling and serious. We were. We traveled, she made friends, a great many friends, women as well as men were amused by her witty tongue, and fascinated by her looks. Four years running, a portrait of her, two of them by the same accomplished bounder, hung in the Academy. She became a patron of the ballet. The life we lived was one it's next to impossible to live now—the amplitude, physical and moral, is missing. . . . The extraordinary thing is, y'know—when I picked her up she was not only uneducated, she had no taste. She dressed vulgarly, she had never opened an intelligent book, nor heard any but the lowest sort of music. Training her gave me the most exquisite pleasure—first to speak well and dress herself, then to look at paintings, hear music, read, admire the right plays, furnish a room, and so on and so forth."

A silence.

"She was very quick, everything—everything I could give her —came easily to her, it was like teaching an eager boy . . . Am I boring you?"

"No," Michal said. But why the devil are you telling me? he wondered. He had an inkling of the reason, and stifled in himself an impulse of affection for the cynical malicious old devil.

"We had fifteen years of this pleasant life . . . In 1935—she was thirty-five, and even then hardly as beautiful as she became in another few months—she asked me to let her divorce me, the man she wanted to marry was a diplomat and didn't care to risk a scandal. I—"

He stopped, smiling, a finely cruel smile, and said reflectively, "If you have ever been tempted to respect a woman, you can

[114]

imagine the—let's say, the gamy flavor of what followed. I should have agreed, of course. But before I had time even to nod or say yes, she had gone on to say that a suit for nullity would be very disagreeable for me—unless I preferred it . . . No doubt this was the first moment I opened my eyes. And I discovered that for years her friends—who were also mine—had been comparing extremely amusing stories about my impotence. Really very amusing . . . I wrote some of them down at the time, to make sure of the details . . . And—well, I did for her out of contempt what I would have done for, let's say, friendship, I allowed her to divorce me with a woman whose name and face I've forgotten completely, my lawyer found her for me. She, my wife, married her diplomat, and has been eminently successful in the part, she has even published a book of memoirs, including the fiction of her birth and upbringing, and hinting with hideous tact at the reason for the failure of her first marriage." He laughed briefly. "So, my friend, now you know what I have been so long writing. My own memoirs. The story of my life and hers—story of a little tart arrested for shoplifting. I went to a great deal of trouble to find out all there is to know about her real parents, a small shopkeeping couple called Roach. A pleasant name. It's all down. I'm leaving the whole thing, with the documents needed to back it up, to be published after my death. This should, in the course of nature, precede hers by at least twenty years. Not long enough for her to have to live with it . . . Well?"

Michal did not speak at once. He took his time about pouring the armagnac into Leighton's glass and his own, turning over in his mind an image of the powerful nearly fleshless head, its arched nose and small piercing ironic eyes, brooding with the most acute pleasure over the phrases that were to destroy the woman who had injured him beyond the possibility of forgiveness.

"You won't have the satisfaction of watching her live with it," he said.

"I can content myself," Leighton said very calmly, "with

thinking about it in my last minutes. A good way to end."

"The book has given you pleasure to write."

"Enormous."

"You couldn't make do with that, and let her off?"

Leighton spoke with brutally amused contempt. "After all, you're a sentimental fellow."

"I don't think so," Michal said. "I understand what you've done. You're bitter—"

The savagery with which Leighton cut him short startled him.

"I have no bitterness. None, none. I'm absolutely indifferent."

"Then why not let her off—if you've forgotten that twenty years ago she made you suffer?"

"I have never suffered," Leighton said violently. "Never. Neither over her nor anyone."

Michal shrugged his shoulders. What was the use of arguing with a man would use every degree of sarcastic brutality to protect himself from his own craving for a little warmth?

"Have you seen her in the last years?"

"No," Leighton said. And after a moment, "About eight years ago she was staying in Villefranche. I thought of going there—not to speak to her, merely catch a glimpse of her, to see how well she was aging. I didn't go." He added in a curious voice, almost young and full, "My God, she was lovely—with her milky skin, and the fine outline of her face—" he moved the dry fingers of one hand, cupping it—"her immense eyes—the way she held herself and moved."

Michal warned himself: Above all, no pity.

"Why have you told me all this?"

The other looked at him with an expression between mockery and a tolerant liking. "Perhaps as a sop to your vanity. Why should I let you think you're the first man to be made a laughingstock by his infatuation? The difference between us is that I learned my lesson. Whether you can is doubtful."

"A mouthful each left," Michal said.

His glass emptied, the Englishman said, "Give me a hand up-

[116]

stairs, I must go home and go to bed. It's damned hard to sleep at my age, y'know."

"Four hours is as long as I need," Michal said carelessly. He stretched his body, easing the muscles of his back.

"Fortunate brute!"

In the empty café, "old nanny goat" was snoring behind the counter, a thread of saliva running from the corner of her blackened lips, her head, its damp quills hanging over her eyes, propped against the edge of a shelf. The Arab watched her as indifferently as he would have watched a dog lying in the sun. Standing up, he took almost into his arms Leighton's frail body, reduced to little more than its bony armature, and as light as a child's.

In the car, Leighton thought again, only very briefly, of giving or lending Michal the money he had lost, and again dismissed the idea.

Somewhere he is a boastful crafty Greek, he told himself lightly; he has other qualities, but he belongs to a world, a life, I know nothing about. Why should I impoverish myself for his benefit? He'll survive. . . . Contrary to local belief, Leighton was no longer a rich man. During the second war—through bad luck, bad management, and a culpable indifference—he had lost three quarters of his money. It was this, not any of the reasons hinted at by one of his few remaining English correspondents, that had sent him to North Africa to live. What he had left—after reasonable provision for Ahmed—would go to the only person who had a right to expect it, a half brother born of his mother's second marriage, a dull decent man he mildly disliked, married, with children . . .

As he expected, he did not sleep. It was not the armagnac, although the quantity he had drunk might well have curdled what juices he still had in his body. It was not even the lees of the excitement which had taken possession of him when he was shuffling together the last pages of his manuscript. At some moment when he was talking to Aristide Michal, a wound had opened in him which he could not close: he tried with both hands to draw its edges together, in terror of its opening wider or deeper . . .

He was in Venice with her—of all banal stage sets for a minute of complete happiness. Between birth and dying a human being is allowed perhaps three or four of these minutes. He had taken her to Torcello, and they came back to Venice across the lagoon at that hour when the light washes from the buildings facing it all corporeal disgrace, all lightest breath of decay, and re-creates them as the closing phrases of one of Mozart's violin concertos. He was trying over in his mind the phrase most nearly identical with the scene when a movement of her arm against his made him glance at her, and he was so pierced by her face and body in the light that he thought he was losing consciousness.

Remembering it, he sat up in his bed in this house he had rented because any solitary house in unmercifully hard country would do, and pushed the blanket from him with yellow bony fingers. Tears came into his eyes.

Such beauty is unbearable, he thought, without knowing what he was thinking.

The same year, was it?, the third or fourth of their marriage, he came home, late in the day, from a fortnight's absence abroad, to find that she was ill. He had not been told. When he went into her room, she was lying in the bed as though she were sinking in it, her body scarcely lifting the blankets. She spoke in a strangely childish voice, full of relief. "Oh, there you are, I've been so frightened." He sat with her half the night, and held one of her hands, while she slept quietly. He did not dare to move. He had never known such deep calm tenderness.

After the divorce, when he was paying her maid of that time to talk to him about her, he learned that the illness was a miscarriage. Queerly, the two things, the emotion of that one night and the sour humiliating truth, existed in his memory entirely separated from one another.

Moving with effort, he put his legs over the side of the bed and stood up, feeling the prick of the acid in his joints when they took the weight, little as that was, of his body.

The shutters of the window were closed. He pushed them open, and the April night came into the room with its scent of herbs and cold earth. Outside, the last quarter of the moon hardly thinned the darkness sliding between the branches of the cypress. Only in the far distance was there enough milky light in the sky to define a bristling line of mountains.

The worst thing in the world, he thought, would be to forget, forget everything.

You old ape, he mocked himself brutally, you know what she was—a young woman with the instincts of a healthy lively bitch.

He groaned lightly.

Light as the sound was, Ahmed, sleeping on the other side of a partition wall, heard it. He came in, and half carried Leighton back to the bed, laying him on his side so that he could stroke the sunken back of his neck. The light pressure of his fingers, very cool, very hard, gradually penetrated to Leighton's spine and brain, and he slept.

Pulling the blanket up round him, Ahmed withdrew as noiselessly as he had come.

11

Luc-Albert Gaudo's position in the neighborhood had always been a tribute to the man rather than to his function. Nor did it rest solely on his reputation as an orator, still less as a man of letters, a term used by the more adroit of his flatterers. His ugly powerful body, less powerful now that its organs were beginning to pay the cost of years of overindulgence of all his senses, sheltered a dangerously lively and oversensitized heart, which despised nearly everybody he knew (including the men and women who had been his benefactors when he was a young man)—not out of malice but from disappointment. He was revolted—the word is not strong enough—by cruelty and hypocrisy, and in one way and another he had been forced to see that both serve the commonest human pleasures. Once he had accepted this fact, he fell back on the one sure consolation he knew: the use of power.

Any man who wants more than anything in the world to be powerful taps in himself an energy of the devil. It was this, this alarming spiritual voltage, and not his intelligence, not even his truly magnificent eloquence, that imposed itself on other people, on his equals as quickly as on subordinates and—which is more remarkable in the closed society of a provincial town—on his social superiors.

The examining magistrate, Monsieur Charles-Bernard Garuche, belonged to an old very respected family, connected on all sides with the small nobility of the district. He was a young man, not long out of college, intelligent and very ambitious, and possessed of a charm he knew very well how to use on older people. In his well-cared-for hand he had every trump needed to enable him to look down his pointed nose at the son of Albert Gaudo, butcher. But he was as much dominated by the older man as if he had been one of Gaudo's admiring terrorized subordinates, and was prepared to let him play out his official role to its limit and beyond. With apparent patience he would wait for Gaudo to bring him the complete file of a case, with or without a signed confession. And although usually he stood on his right to be present when the police were examining witnesses in an affair, nine times out of ten he never opened his mouth. This was not timidity. He was not timid, he was only naturally and excessively prudent. He was learning all the time. The saying, "Better a magistrate than the police," implied many things. At this stage of his career one of its implications might be only his lack of experience and personal force. He had no intention of allowing his ambition to show until he were a little more certain of not being destined to kick his heels for years in a subprefecture magistrate's court. Meantime he courted Gaudo as he courted everyone in his path, young, old, rich, weak, powerful.

For the past six weeks Gaudo's failure to get anywhere in the Aristide Michal case had been a daylong delight to him; he smiled at it over his morning coffee, over his claret at dinner, and in his mistress's bedroom.

This morning, in the office on the ground floor of the Town Hall, he confronted a Gaudo sweating certainties from every pore.

"Every day for a month I've been expecting this."

The young magistrate smiled deferentially. "What, exactly?"

"That the young sinner would bolt. What still puzzles me a little is why he waited a month. No doubt some arrangement with the others. And now we shan't be long. Any man who really wants to hide himself can, even for years, but not a young idiot—and not with that face."

"Tell me something. Were you sure at the beginning that the boy was involved?"

"No," Gaudo said. His vanity, which was colossal, did not extend to lying about his intellect. "I really thought it possible that it was an accident. That two young louts had planned, only during dinner, when they found that a woman was in charge, to take what money, much or little, there was in the place, if it was only the takings of one day, and being louts, they started by brutalizing the woman and came on the safe then. That was my first notion. But I began, quite soon, to smell something gamier."

"How soon?"

"To tell you the truth—I don't mind telling the truth, why should I?—it was a day in the first week when I went there to question the old woman, Thérèse What's-it. After lunch I thought I'd look at the kitchen again, and Master Philippe's room. I was standing in the doorway of his room, not looking for anything, just looking, and he was behind me. When I moved my head a fraction I saw him reflected in a glass on a wall of the room, and just then Madame Michal, let's call her Madame Michal, came into the kitchen, and gave him a look. They were both behind my back, and she had no idea I could see her. Well, if ever I saw a woman sunk above her eyes in an infatuated obsession, I was seeing it then. I realized that she'd shield him with her own body from a machine gun, and I thought: She's been lying."

The magistrate wrinkled his nose in the boyish smile that had charmed so many people. "Surely you don't think—" He spread his hands out.

"I think that by then—I say: by then—she knew he knew something. If he hadn't been in it himself, he knew the two fellows who were and he meant to get his cut. And that—at the moment—is as far as I go."

"Madame Michal," Garuche murmured, "is a fine-looking woman. But she's not a young woman."

"Fifty-five! What age is that? She's by way of being his mother, but she could have a more than motherly feeling for him, eh?"

"You shock me," the magistrate said calmly.

"My God, you don't know men and women. The most mediocre, the noblest, the most, let's say, well-meaning, have their hours. Of destruction—if you like, self-destruction."

"I find it difficult to imagine—" the magistrate began.

He broke off as the door opened: his own secretary came in, to say that the Michals, husband and wife, were in the anteroom.

"Bring them in, please."

He stood up as they entered, although he did not hold out his hand.

"Please sit down, Madame Michal. Forgive us for bringing you here, but . . ."

Lotte looked at him without a smile. She had made up more heavily than usual; the long lines of her mouth were exaggerated by the blackish crimson she had laid on too thickly. Her hair, which she had brushed down over her forehead almost to her eyes, and behind her ears, had the gleam of melting pitch.

"Of course."

"You, too, Monsieur Michal," the magistrate said, sitting down behind his table.

Gaudo had contented himself with a nod of the head at Lotte. Settling himself comfortably, he looked at Monsieur Garuche.

"Do you wish to ask some questions?"

"No, no," the magistrate said, smiling faintly. "I shall leave it to you."

"Monsieur Michal," Gaudo began, with genial politeness. He

took Michal, step by seemingly haphazard step, from the day when he adopted a child who had, it appeared, been abandoned, to the moment when he came back from Nice with five million francs in a borrowed suitcase.

"When you went into Nice that morning in March, you had no intention of coming home with a bag full of money?"

"No, of course not," Michal said heavily. Mortified by being reminded of his folly, he scowled at the policeman.

"And you told no one—I mean, except your wife—that you had it?"

"No one. I told you that at the time."

"You are still sure? No one in the village, and no one, except Maître Jouassaint, in Nice?"

"Of course I am sure. I am an ass but not a talking ass."

"I am the ass who talks," Gaudo said affably.

He asked another round of questions, all of which, in one form or another, he had asked before this. Then, lowering his voice to one of its deeper levels,

"You have had, perhaps, during the years, reasons to complain a little of your son—we'll call him your son, it's simpler—before this trick of running away? Boys will be boys, eh?"

"Never," Michal said.

The feeling of desolation and bewilderment that spread through him was a bodily pain. He gripped the edges of his chair.

"Ah. In short—you did not know him so well as you imagined you did. Not so well as your wife knew him."

Without glancing at Lotte, Michal moved his head, lowering it, from side to side, to ease the muscles of his neck. He did not answer.

"I wonder which of us knows our children," Gaudo said in a pathetic voice. He was childless. He turned to Lotte. "Tell me when it was you began to suspect that the boy, that your son—" he laid a light stress on the word—"was leading a somewhat dubious life outside the hotel and the village."

"At no time," Lotte said dryly.

Narrowing her eyes, she straightened herself in her chair. This, perhaps, was the moment she had been waiting for, when the dangerous animal confronting them would turn from Michal to threaten her.

"Ah. Well, we shall come back to that in a minute. First, I am going to read to you from the statement Philippe made when he came here after the robbery. . . . Give me the papers," he said rudely. Taking them from the secretary without thanks, he read out the passage in which, asked when he had learned that the money was in the safe, Philippe said: On the Tuesday—and went on to explain why he remembered that it was Tuesday and not Saturday or any other day.

"You see?" Gaudo said. "He was quite sure and quite frank. Why do you go on insisting that he mistook the day?"

Looking at him with a sarcastic smile, Lotte said,

"What's easy to see is that you're determined to prove I'm lying."

"Oh, come now, come now, Madame Michal. Why should you lie? Mistaken—you could be making a mistake. And another thing. You were certain, you told us, that during the whole of the evening Philippe was never out of the kitchen and did not see the young men who came to dine and asked for a bed for the night. But old Thérèse is also sure that he left the kitchen for at least five minutes, and her impression at the time was that he went up the stairs and stood there looking into the café where the two were now sitting drinking. But perhaps you had your back turned to him the whole of the five minutes? Eh?"

"Thérèse is an old woman."

"And your Philippe is a very young man. But they both have bad memories." His smile was full of shrewdness and good-fellowship. "You are a noble mother, Madame Michal, you defend your young before they are attacked."

The blood rose slowly under Lotte's thick olive-tawny skin, to her cheekbones, to her forehead. She drew her thick eyebrows together, staring at her tormentor as she might have looked at a cockroach under her foot. Michal knew the signs, she was losing her temper and might say anything.

"And if I do?" she said, in her deepest voice.

"To defend too soon is as bad as not to defend at all," Gaudo said, still smiling. "Y'know, you are making a mistake."

"Have it your own way," she said violently. "It was Tuesday, Wednesday, Thursday, Friday—I don't remember. You can choose the day that suits your filthiest ideas."

The young magistrate leaned across the table. His voice sounded embarrassed. "Madame Michal, you are not here to be irritated into saying anything you don't mean. Are you now quite sure that you don't remember on which day of the week—"

Lotte cut him short. "Yes. *I don't remember.*"

"Then why did you . . . ?"

"Because I knew that you, or Monsieur Gaudo, would try to lay a trap for him."

"And since you knew he was innocent—at least innocent of theft," Gaudo said, "you thought he would be sure to walk blindly into any trap a wicked man set up. Innocence, defenseless innocence, eh?"

Unable to sit quiet any longer, Aristide Michal said,

"You might remind yourself that the thugs you haven't managed to catch yet reduced my wife to a state when she might confuse anything."

In his heart of hearts he did not believe this, but to provoke Gaudo gave him a little relief.

"Be quiet," Gaudo said sharply. He turned back to Lotte. "Are you still sure he didn't come upstairs to look at the two men? It's not another of your mistakes?"

She had recovered her self-control. "I'm absolutely sure," she said coldly and quietly. "Thérèse has a head like a colander, she won't remember her own funeral—and I have no doubt you frightened her. The boy had nothing to do with the robbery." With an air of wanting to make any reasonable concession, she

[126]

added, "At the worst he might, if he really did know about it in time, have talked to someone in Nice or Marseilles or elsewhere about the money. But it's not likely. He's not a fool."

"I am not sure that he is a fool," Gaudo said, speaking amiably, "but he is certainly not a good boy, he has been sleeping about the place with these fatuous old women—what is it *happens* with women when they move themselves from north to south?—for what he could get out of them, and with young ones for other reasons." He stretched his gross body forward, to look into Lotte's face. "And you didn't know anything about his amusements, eh, Madame Michal?"

"I don't now," she said coolly.

"Ah. You are very very fond of him, eh?"

"Yes."

"So fond of him you didn't mind deceiving your husband about his extravagance, you gave him money, and you didn't tell your husband: The boy is spending a lot of money these days . . . Why didn't you tell him?"

Lotte's smile said: You're less clever than you think. "It's easy to see you haven't had children. I didn't want him to be angry with the boy."

"Didn't you think sometimes that you were doing a wrong thing?"

"I—" she hesitated—"it didn't seem very important."

"You were fonder of Philippe than of your husband—was that it, eh?"

"No," Lotte said harshly.

She glanced at the young magistrate, as if inviting him to come to her help, but although he looked uncomfortable, and fidgeted with his blotting pad, aligning it carefully with the edge of the table, he did not speak.

Biting her lip, she lifted a hand to her forehead. It was damp with sweat under the thick fold of hair, and a thin trickle was beginning on one temple. Her moment of self-confidence had weakened her.

Gaudo leaned back. "I wish I understood you. You rob your husband—I take it that when he gave you money he did not say: This is to spend on Philippe—and you keep from him things you knew about the boy that a sensible responsible-minded woman would have told him at once. But you are a sensible woman . . . What sort of unwise infatuated feeling is this you had for the boy? To make you behave in the same way as these old women who should know better. Well—I mean, behave as idiotically."

After a moment, Lotte said with contempt,

"What else do you want to know?"

"I have finished for the time," he said harshly. "Unless Monsieur le Juge has anything he wants to ask you, you can go."

The magistrate shook his head.

Alone with the Commissioner, he said in a voice he made cool and admiring,

"You drove her very near an edge of some sort."

"Poor woman," Gaudo said.

The warmth, the bitter sincerity, in his voice took the younger man sharply aback, and wiped off his face the fine smile he allowed himself when he was both amused and inquisitive. Especially the warmth surprised him. As Gaudo had said, he did not know a great deal about people . . .

On the drive home, Michal did not speak. He felt Lotte's glance on him, and deliberately avoided meeting it. Since the day before, in fact since the moment when she turned on him and asked him to leave her alone, he had done just that, coming to bed long after she was uneasily asleep, and in the morning leaving her with her coffee and drinking his own in the kitchen, at the stove. There was no hostility in his silence: it was, simply, that he had not yet assimilated what he had been told about the boy. It lay in his mind like a stone, he knocked himself against it again and again, with the same stupefaction, the same bile. For the time being he had no energy to spare for her and her grief and deceit. His own humiliation absorbed, paralyzed, him. His flesh itched from the glances of pity, half-deliberate malice, and superstitious avoidance—as if he might bring ill-luck—that met him in the village. If he could have taken one of these glances by the throat and strangled it . . . but neither his rage nor his grief had any outlet.

It was not yet five when they got back to the Hotel Moderne Aristide. Lotte went directly to their bedroom, and shut the door. Standing fingering his mustache in the empty café, he allowed himself a moment of lucidity, of puerile astonishment. "Can it be happening?" He had an impulse to talk to Lotte, but it was too feeble to carry him across the room and he was about to go downstairs to the kitchen when the door opened sharply. She stood there looking at him for a moment.

"Come here," she said quietly.

It was so nearly the voice she had used to call to him from a dark stinking passage in Marseilles, thirty years ago, that he heard it with the same start of blood in his veins. Walking toward her, he said,

"What do you want?"

"Only to talk to you."

He came into the room, closing the door. "What is it?"

She had seated herself on the side of the bed. "You are blaming me," she said humbly.

Am I? he asked himself. Yes, a little. "Only for not warning me that the boy was asking you for money. I might have done something. Found out—at least—what he was spending it on—the sort of life."

"Do you believe all that?"

"What? What d'you mean?"

She passed her tongue over her lips. "Those women."

"My God, how can I tell? I don't know yet what I believe."

"There are so many things he might have needed money for. A good-looking boy—he had a great many friends—nowadays money slips through your fingers like water."

[129]

He remembered the little tart, Rouché, and her scrannel voice. "That girl who was here—"

"No, don't let's talk about her," Lotte said, with a cold violence. "I can't stand it. Not after what we've just had. That brute Gaudo . . ."

"Very well." He felt restless: all the energy in his powerful body, an animal ready to tumble one way into anger or another into any sort of activity, seemed to have turned against himself, he wanted to use his hands against someone, to go out and walk rapidly somewhere, anywhere, to put his head back and bellow, like a tethered bull. "You wanted to talk," he said, "tell me something. *Why* didn't you warn me?"

For a moment she didn't answer him. Then again she made use of that same penetrating voice, deep, flexible, oddly impersonal in its seduction, as heartlessly poignant as a bird's.

"I didn't want you to be hurt."

"Is that all you were worrying about? Not about Philippe?"

"Oh—" she smiled briefly—"I wanted him to have everything he wanted. Of course. But—more than anything—I wanted you to feel happy about him. You were happy, you know. And I thought . . . I thought that in a year or two he would settle down—as young men do settle down when . . ."

She pressed her hand over her eyes. She is terribly ashamed, he thought. He also thought, shrewdly, that she must have learned some extremely bitter truths about herself during the last day or two, perhaps during the last weeks. Her vanity is hurt, he thought. Because his own had taken this severe beating, he did not make the error of belittling the torments of mortally hurt vanity. They may not be noble, he said to himself, but they are singularly lasting, and rank second, I daresay, to the feeling of hopeless loss, a death or what have you.

He pushed everything out of his mind except the wish to comfort her.

"Don't blame yourself," he said, with great simplicity, "being overkind isn't a fault. It can be a blunder but it's not a fault."

"You're the most generous person I know," Lotte said, in a low voice.

"No," he said, smiling. "It costs me nothing to give away certain things. Money is dirt. Other things"—he did not give himself the trouble to glance at them, but they included his reputation as a splendid cook and his standing in whatever community he had to live in—"I should resent being robbed of."

She did not look at him. "Forgive me for being a disappointment."

He touched her face lightly. "Y'know, they won't be long finding the boy, and we'll get things cleared up. Don't worry."

The sound she made was near enough being a whimper to startle him. She cut it short, and smiled at him.

"One thing," she said, with an effort. "I respect and admire you more than anyone in the world, I always did and always shall."

He believed her. He believed her easily—with his vanity and his heart. Paradoxically, at this moment he recalled the Englishman's intolerant grating voice: Are you sure you know everything now? . . . His vanity or his restless energy answered for him: What the hell more is there to know? And since I have as much cleverness and strength as I need . . .

Almost thoughtlessly, he began to caress her, stroking her neck and undoing the buttons of her blouse to get at the cleft between her heavy breasts, still firm. Nowadays it was not often that his sexual need of her was so pressing and violent as it became, suddenly. At first this body he was lying over remained almost rigid, but after a moment or two it softened, opening to him with a kind of desperation. He laid a finger on the mole. She shuddered. Speaking against his mouth, she said under her breath, "He must have noticed it when he was a little boy, one isn't always careful then."

"Will you be quiet?" he said.

[131]

12

Overconfident as often, Gaudo had given Philippe a run of two weeks at the longest. In fact it was a full month—the end of May—before he was picked up, almost accidentally, in Paris. Three young men, all more or less drunk, began a savage quarrel in the basement night club off the Place Pigalle where they were already known, from their accent and manners, as Marseilles types. They were not regular customers at a place no seedier or more commonplace than a dozen others they might have dropped on, but they had been in several times, with or without women. This evening they were without, they came in at midnight in a state of noisy excitement which in three or four hours turned sour. One of them had been accusing the others of cheating him out of his rightful share of a specific sum of money, and as soon as it came to the stage of overturning tables and breaking a bottle to use the edge, the proprietor and his doorman fell on them and threw them into the street. But before this, he had been listening with more attention than he usually gave to a drunken argument, and next morning—he was a man who both needed and liked to keep one hand in with the police—repeated as much as he had heard to the inspector who happened to be calling on him. He knew, too, whereabouts in the neighborhood one of the three, a handsome young fellow, was living.

As soon as they had identified him, the police sent Philippe back to Grasse. He had answered all their questions with the reckless indifference they were used to in amateur or apprentice criminals, and told them where they would be nearly certain to pick up the other two, who might, he believed, be on their way to Italy, but were unlikely to have left Paris.

(He was mistaken. It was five weeks before they were caught, in a bungled robbery, in Lyons.)

In his hotel room and his pocket, Philippe had between two and three thousand francs. He told the police that when he arranged with his two friends in Marseilles to break into the safe, it had been agreed to divide the money equally, one half to him, the other to be shared between two. But, he said petulantly, when he turned up to claim his half they put him off with less than a third. They had been living it up, not too imprudently, first in Lyons, then in Paris, and he was, they told him, lucky to have that much to pick up. They made him various promises, none of which they could keep. Nor, if you want to enjoy yourself a little, does money go very far in a bastard of a city like Paris . . .

When he rang Michal to tell him to come to Grasse, and bring his wife, Gaudo told him no more than that they had Philippe. The rest of the story he told them in somewhat brutal detail when they were sitting, side by side on an uncomfortable wooden settle, in his room at the police station. Once or twice he broke off the narrative and waited, as though giving them the chance to ask a question. One of these pauses fell when he was describing the way Philippe had lived in Paris. "Young louts," he growled, "like these three, not professional criminals yet, are also invariably fools—their one notion about money is to spend

[133]

it, as idiotically as possible." Neither of his listeners spoke. Watching him fixedly, one hand doubled under her full greedy chin, Lotte might have been listening abstractedly in the café to one of Monsieur Pibourdin's half-true half-malicious anecdotes.

Michal felt nothing more than the familiar stupefying bewilderment, a mutter at the back of his head of can-it-be-true?, cut off at moments by physical giddiness.

At last, heaving himself out of his chair, Gaudo said he was taking them to the examining magistrate, and he thought: We're going to see him. . . . The relief when, lifting his head as he came into the room, he saw that Philippe was not there, was so overwhelming that for the first time he had the energy to think of Lotte. Glancing at her, he thought: My God, this is hard on her. . . . But he expected her to be able to stand it. If he could, why not she?

Monsieur Garuche was at pains to be very polite, ceremonious, with Lotte. He came round his table to place her in a chair, inquired whether the sun was in her eyes, and had his clerk fuss with the blinds.

It seemed that they were to have read to them parts of the statement Philippe had made, the day before, in this room. Looking at them with a benevolence which, coming from a young man, was very attractive, the magistrate said,

"You know, I think, already, that the accused"—the term caught Michal in the pit of his stomach, wrenching it—"has admitted to arranging, with two young men known to him—since we haven't yet laid hands on them we have not had their story —to rob his father, his, ah, adoptive father, of money he knew to be in the safe. Here is the passage dealing with this . . . *When she*—" pausing, the young judge said, with charming diffidence, "I must tell you, Madame Michal, that throughout this statement the accused refers to you as *Ti*—I take it that he was accustomed to speaking to and of you by this name . . ."

Lotte's only response was to close her eyes for a moment.

"Well—I'll go on, shall I? *When she told me, on Tuesday,*

*that the money was in the safe, and by the way it was Tuesday
she told me, not Saturday, the silly creature didn't warn me she
was going to make it Saturday, I thought it was the chance I'd
been waiting for, to get away . . ."* Turning over three or more
pages rapidly, he said, "Details of what he said to his accom-
plices, and their replies, are not in this connection very important. Coming to the Saturday evening—he describes what we
know happened, the arrival of the young men after dusk, putting
the car away, dining, drinking in the café, asking for a room, and
the rest. Then he goes on—please listen carefully—*I had fixed it
with Ti to let herself be roped up and I did the job properly.
In fact I overdid it a bit, she—*"

The interruption he was expecting came in a voice lower
than he expected, but so sonorous that it would have been audi-
ble through an uproar.

"He is lying."

Laying the sheet of paper down, the magistrate looked at her
with nothing more than curiosity in the eyes, a pale limpid blue,
fringed thickly with colorless lashes, which the mothers of mar-
riageable girls had the habit of speaking about as "charming
but so reserved."

"You were, though, tied to the bed, very roughly?"

Lotte returned his glance without any uneasiness. "Yes. But
the rest is lies—all lies."

"Will you tell us what happened?"

"If you want me to," she said dryly. "It's only what I told
Monsieur Gaudo and he had it written down, and I signed it."

"Be kind enough to tell me now."

"The two young men—I'd never seen them before that evening, when I served them myself—came into my bedroom some
time during the night when I was asleep, and one of them held
me with his hand over my mouth while the other went through
all the drawers until he found the keys. Then, after they'd taken
the money, they tied me to the bed by my wrists and ankles,
and pushed a chemise they took off the floor into my mouth, and

tied a stocking around that, and went away." She shuddered and closed her eyes. "It was horrible."

"You were taken entirely by surprise," the magistrate said gently.

"Of course."

"And you saw only the two men. Your—your son, Philippe, was not in the room?"

"No—not until he came in in the morning."

"Then he is lying when he says he fastened you to the bed? And that you knew he meant to take the money that night and had agreed to the whole criminal affair, including the rough treatment of yourself?"

Dropping her voice again, she said, very slowly,

"Certainly he is lying."

"Can you—" he paused—"can you suggest his reason for telling us this story?"

Lotte seemed to hesitate. "A reason? No."

The sound Gaudo made scraping his chair on the polished boards startled her. She turned her head. He had been sitting, sprawled, looking up at the ceiling, as though to make very plain his status in this room as an onlooker. Now he bent himself forward, thighs widely parted, a hand on each broad knee, in the pose characteristic of him, so his subordinates said, when he smelled blood.

"Will you allow me, Monsieur le Juge?" he said loudly. Without any polite pause, he went on, "The reason could be that it is true, as a whole and in detail. I am speaking only to you, Madame Michal, not to your husband, do not look at him— look at me, I am going to go over these *details* with you . . ."

At this moment, Aristide Michal remembered that Leighton had warned him of the unwisdom of putting your unguarded hand between the jackal's teeth. I could stop it now, he thought uncertainly, I could tell her not to answer, to wait until we have Jouassaint here, to wait . . . Nothing, no force in the world, certainly not the glance Lotte sent him, of appeal or only anguish, would induce him to wait. Looking back at her steadily, he thought: Whatever there is to know, I want to know it at once. . . .

"When the two men entered your room you were asleep?"

"Yes."

"Their entry was a shock, and it surprised you?"

"Yes."

"It was not part of the arrangement you had with Philippe?"

"There was no arrangement," Lotte said. "I made none."

"You deny that he came into the room along with the two men?"

"Yes."

"Before he bolted a month ago, you did not suspect him of having a hand in the robbery—is that what you ask us to believe?"

"Why not? It is the truth."

"He has confessed to the robbery. But you insist, you still insist that he kept out of sight completely, didn't come in to give them a hand, and point out the safe. You'll agree it doesn't seem likely."

"He was never in the room."

"And you insist that it wasn't he who tied you up and gagged you—so effectively that you could neither move nor scream?"

"How could he have done it? He was not there."

Abruptly, Gaudo began to use the voice, deep, powerful, brutally sarcastic, he kept for the critical moments of an examination. The young magistrate winced and kept his head down like a man protecting himself in an east wind.

"Any young man might dislike having to confess that he had used physical cruelty on his mother. And might deny it if he were accused. But here we have a young fellow who doesn't wait to be accused before he admits it. What d'you say to that, eh, Madame Michal?"

Staring at him, Lotte said evenly,

"I say he is lying."

[137]

"You yourself, I may remind you, told us lies about the day of the week when he first heard from you that the money had been left in the safe."

"No. I got the days confused. Is that a crime?"

"You lied, as long as it was possible to lie, about Philippe's raffish life, and about having given him the money for it. Answer, please."

"If it is a question—yes."

"But you are not lying when you tell us that he did not show himself in the bedroom? And did not brutalize you?"

"Those are not lies."

"Come now, Madame Michal, have you any idea why he should be anxious to persuade us that he behaved worse than he did—if you are not still lying to us?"

She was silent.

Gaudo moved his chair again, bringing him so near her that she must have felt his breath on her cheek, and felt that his shoulders, his enormous face, the stretch of his long moist upper lip, his small pig's eyes with their perpetual tiny flame, were lying over her.

"You'll not deny that—of all the details in which his admissions contradict yours—this is the least plausible, the least sane."

No, I can't stand this, Michal thought. He stood up, his mouth opened to order, "Stop this," but even before he could get it out, Lotte broke. He thought she was going to put her hands over her ears, but all she did was hold them, doubled, on a level with her face.

"He was there, yes. And he tied me to the bed—yes, yes, yes."

Michal heard her voice—*They needn't have been so rough.* Speaking to Philippe, who had done it, he thought. To a fellow thief. *No!*

"Ah," Gaudo breathed.

He leaned back, looking at her with an expression devoid of any emotion, even of satisfaction.

"Then the rest of your story is a lie," he said, in his every-day voice, heavy and not unpleasant. "You knew what would happen that night. You helped to plan it and lent yourself to the pretense of a robbery by two thugs. You—"

Lotte cut him short. "No." She was colorless, with a film of sweat over her forehead and chin, but she had her voice in control again. "I didn't plan anything. I was"—she paused, looking down at the hands now lying in her lap—"horrified."

Gaudo almost smiled. "And do you expect anyone, me, the judges, your husband, anyone, to believe that that is not another lie?"

"I don't expect anything from you but more bullying," she said with contempt.

"Well, well, my dear good woman, there is one fact you won't deny. Even you. From that night onward at any rate, you knew the boy was guilty of theft. Whatever else you didn't know, or you profess not to have known, you knew that. Eh?"

She nodded.

"But you held your tongue. Why?"

"I—" she hesitated—"I was afraid."

"For yourself?"

"I was afraid of what my husband would do to Philippe."

Gaudo raised his eyebrows above menacing eyes. "So you were willing to let your husband lose all his savings, all he had, the hotel, all, rather than tell us who was responsible—at a time when there was more than a chance of getting the money back before it vanished. Answer."

"Yes, I was," she said in her lowest voice. Aristide Michal made an inarticulate sound, but she did not look at him. "I was sorry for him, for my husband. I didn't want him to know. He loved Philippe so much . . . I tell you, I was sorry."

"A good way to show your sorrow," Gaudo said. He went on easily, "And now, Madame Michal, to show you that I am not a bully, I will give you one chance. One last little chance. You have heard what Philippe says, you don't want me to read it

[139]

again? No? Well, he tells us he fixed everything with you beforehand, to take the money, the way it was to be done, everything. Is this a lie? Come now, you'll feel better and happier,
you'll even feel freer, if you tell us the whole truth—whatever
it costs you. Y'know, sometimes it's a relief to be punished!"

"Lotte—" Michal said.

She looked at him, not at Gaudo. "I've behaved badly, very
very badly. I let you be robbed. But I didn't arrange it, I didn't
think he would do that to you. How could I, how could I know
that he, that Philippe . . ."

She had been speaking in a hoarse weak voice, and now it
failed her altogether. She put both hands over her face.

"I'll take her home," Michal said. He took a step toward her.

Gaudo waved a sergeant-major's hand at him. "Yes, yes. But
first we will see the boy, eh?"

He looked at the magistrate. He in turn looked at his secretary who had been absorbedly writing at a table facing the
magistrate's larger table, and the man got up and went out.

He didn't have to be told what to do, Michal thought. The
pressure in his head and body had become unendurable, as
though nerves, veins, every member, were swollen to the point
of bursting. At the sight of Philippe, all this rage and agony did
burst. For a moment he could scarcely see the boy through the
mist of blood behind his eyes; this cleared and he saw him
exactly as he had always been, the look of purity and sensual
delicacy, the arched forehead and finely curved mouth under
the youthful mustache, the eyes, gray and as clear as clear
water.

It was too much. To be so beautiful and so rotten. He lifted
his arms and roared,

"You, what have you been doing? I'll thrash you within an
inch of your life, I'll—"

To his astonishment and dismay, tears ran down his face, and
he choked into silence.

Philippe looked at him with a comical expression of embarrassment. "Oh, don't take it like that, dad," he said. "I'm sorry, I wish I hadn't done it, it was pretty stupid. How stupid can you get? I should have waited."

"You must control yourself, you know, Monsieur Michal," the magistrate said coolly and kindly. "And sit down, please." He turned to the young man. "Wait." Then for a minute or two he addressed himself to Michal, as though he were trying, out of kindness, to help him pull himself together by making him listen to a wordy explanation of why it was necessary to confront Philippe with "a witness whose evidence shows a discrepancy, I may say a serious discrepancy, with his own statement. You understand, I think, Monsieur Michal, that I, that we, are only anxious to get at the truth, and to help you by getting at it . . . I am going . . ."

Michal ceased to hear the smooth pleasantly courteous voice running like a tap. He was watching Lotte. From the moment Philippe entered, she had been sitting as if she were very cold, shoulders and eyebrows drawn together, eyes narrowed. She did not look at the young man, but stared directly in front of her at a point not in the room. But she was listening—he knew that by a trick she had, when he was giving her instructions about something, of seeming to count the items off on her fingers, pressing them one after another on the table or against her knee. She was doing it now.

He fell into a ludicrous daydream that they were in the kitchen of the Hotel Moderne Aristide, discussing the dinners for the week, and came to himself with a shock to hear Philippe speaking.

". . . of course she knew what was being planned, I told you so. It wasn't her idea, it was mine, and at first she wasn't too keen. But I brought her round and—"

"You're lying," Lotte said. She gave a little dry cough, and said again, "You're lying."

Even now she did not glance at him. He looked at her for a moment with a slight smile before saying,

"Well, Ti, I'm sorry I gave you away, but you know how it is, they go on at you, these flics, until you tell them the truth only to get a minute's peace."

She turned to look at him, her eyes gleaming with anger or some other strong emotion. "Then why not have told them the real truth? Why didn't you tell them that the first thing I knew about it was when you and your two friends came into the room and you asked me for the key? Why?"

Still with the same slight smile, Philippe shrugged his shoulders and, glancing at the magistrate, said,

"She's lying, but what can I do?"

"Coward," Lotte said in her Marseilles voice, "coward, liar. You should be ashamed."

The magistrate coughed, to hide that this voice disquieted him a little. Drawing a sheet of paper toward him, he asked Philippe a question about the sort of life he had led in Nice during the past year. Philippe answered readily, almost merrily, a number of questions about the women he slept with, young, middle-aged and older, very young prostitutes like Rouché, "poor Rouché," and what he called "the respectable old trouts" staying in the fashionable hotels.

"They were the best," he said, smiling, "or the worst, depending how you look at it, rolling over with their old stomachs in the air like cats asking you to scratch them. Pouh!"

His eyes sparkled. Obviously—obvious to his listeners—his easy successes had flattered him, feeding a conceit that was partly youthful and partly, since after all he had made the trouts pay for his attentions, vicious.

This conceit first sickened Michal, then made him think that he had never known the boy. There was no relation between his outward self and his talk: an unknown, ugly and pitiful, was talking. The shock steadied Michal and brought his everyday shrewdness to the surface. He realized suddenly that something, some line of action, had been plotted between the examining magistrate and Gaudo. What the magistrate had in front of him was a list of questions he was reading off—drawn up by the Commissioner? The sense of danger he had had earlier returned, and he thought: I was a prize ass not to have the lawyer here . . . Since it was Philippe who was being questioned now, not Lotte, where, he asked himself sharply, was the danger coming from? Where could it come from? He began to listen with a strained attention.

The magistrate dropped the subject of women, and asked Philippe why he had not gone off with the money at once, why wait a month?

"The idea," Philippe said readily, "was to make it seem that there was no connection between the two things, between the money and me clearing off." He laughed. "A bit cracked, really, when you come to think."

Taking up another sheet of paper, the magistrate said, "Here is what you stated yesterday—*I had promised Ti to take her with me when I went.*" He waited a minute to allow the words to sink in, then asked, "Had the delay anything to do with Madame Michal? With your promise to her?"

Michal stood up. "Why have you kept this until now?"

"Quiet, please," the magistrate said tartly.

Philippe was smiling—grinning, rather. "With my what?"

"Didn't you intend taking her?"

"Of course not." He laughed, throwing his head back. "Poor old Ti, what on earth should I want with her?" He looked directly at Lotte and said, "You didn't expect me to take you, surely, did you, whatever I may have said?"

Involuntarily, the words jerked from him, Michal said,

"Don't answer, don't say anything."

She had got to her feet and was standing in a strangely lax way, arms hanging, head thrown back, a woman half-consciously offering herself.

"You promised," she said, "you promised again and again. Why shouldn't I have believed you?"

Michal thought: She hasn't a hope, he has no idea what she's talking about, none of it makes any sense to him . . . He glanced at Gaudo. The Commissioner was making no effort to hide his brutal satisfaction in having, once more, proved to himself and others that he could get the better of anyone; people kicked against him, wriggled, did everything not to submit, wept, lied, and in the end he overrode or tricked them. His little eyes flamed with joy.

God damn you, Michal thought.

Turning her head toward him, Lotte said,

"I've been sleeping with him, you know, ever since, oh I don't know, a year. You might as well know—since you know everything else."

He did not move. His only conscious feeling was anxiety to show none. Philippe said gently,

"You're a silly old girl, a silly silly old Ti. Why d'you want to make more trouble for yourself? I didn't tell them that. I wouldn't have." He added, with absurd pitiable conceit, his eyes twinkling, "I know the rules!"

"Didn't you mean any of it, anything you said?"

Coming from the roots of her throat, this toneless voice made its way like a worm to Michal's nerves. She doesn't know she's not alone with him, he thought dully.

"I loved you so. Even if I'd known you were rotten I'd still have loved you. I did everything you wanted, didn't I? You knew I loved you, you knew there has never been anyone else I wanted so much as I want you. You knew. Why have you treated me like this? Tell me why. Explain it to me so that I can understand. Philippe!"

Philippe frowned. "Need you make a show of yourself?"

"Why? Why, why?"

He shrugged his shoulders. "You didn't really expect it to last, did you? Damn it, you're old enough to know better than that."

She was still watching him under half-closed eyelids, but for the first time her face lost its almost stony passivity.

"Yes, you mean that," she said, "I understand that now. I

[144]

should have expected it, I should have known you are heartless, I—I—"

Her agony had no effect on the young man except to bring on his handsome face a look of boredom.

"My dear Ti," he said, "haven't we had enough of this? It's no use, you know."

She took a step toward him, wavered, and collapsed on the ground, weeping hoarsely, arms stretched out, the sides of her body heaving like an exhausted dog's. Michal did not move. He could not, she horrified him: the spectacle she was offering them of raw female lust made him shudder. It was Gaudo and the clerk, dropping his pen, who bent over her and helped her to her feet.

"Come now, come now," Gaudo encouraged her, "pull yourself together, no one's dead."

Speaking with cold distaste, the magistrate said,

"It would be a waste of time to attempt to go on now, with Madame Michal in this state. Her husband had better take her away."

Not at all certain that he could bring himself to touch her, Michal moved stiffly, but she was already walking toward the door and when he reached her she made a light gesture keeping him off. He glanced over his shoulder at Philippe. The young man was looking after them with a nearly imperceptible smile, not in the least disturbed, apparently very slightly amused by the scene.

My God, thought Michal, is *this* human nature? Can't anyone be trusted?

On the way home he let the torrent of bewilderment in his mind take possession of him to such a point that he was all but oblivious of the woman sitting beside him. That any young creature could be, as Philippe seemed, completely indifferent to the effects of his actions, struck him as a sort of blasphemy, very hard to accept as possible, let alone understand. After a time he began in a confused way to think that for the last ten or more years he had been making Philippe the center, the deep center, of his life, pushing Lotte a little to one side, not deliberately but by an unconscious choice.

Then is all this my fault? he asked himself.

He rejected the thought instantly. If his loving pride in the boy had made Philippe what he had turned out to be, there was no meaning in life, his own or any. The only thing he could now do was close his mind savagely over this absence of meaning and live with what remained within his grasp.

Telling himself this, he had a moment of astonishing exhilaration.

As she got out of the car Lotte stumbled, and fell on one knee. He let her pick herself up unaided and go in. Suddenly she was only the cause of his humiliation, sickening. When he went into the hotel she was standing outside the door of their room, apparently waiting for him. A black rage seized him, swelling the muscles at the side of his neck. He said coldly,

"Do you need Thérèse to do anything for you?"

"No," she said, "I—"

He turned away and went to the kitchen. Toward time for dinner he opened the door of the bedroom. She was sitting doing nothing.

"Do you mean to stay here all evening?" he asked.

"What do you want me to do?"

"What you always do, of course—serve the tables."

"Yes, yes," she said quietly, "I'll change my dress."

The restaurant that evening was overfull. He preferred it when the eight tables held only couples, or one serious-minded gourmet, but there were four parties tonight of three people and one of four, and it was close on eleven o'clock when he went upstairs to take "old nanny goat's" place at the bar. She was as drunk as an owl. Her eyes had sunk to the back of her skull; her lips, inexplicably blackened, had began to laugh silently and talk to themselves. She was smelling like a whole cage of wild beasts, and when she had to hand over a glass she held it high above her head to get it across some barrier she saw. When Michal sent her off, this barrier rose in front of her and she drew back. "Can't do it," she muttered, "this time I'm done, they've got me, the swine." He took her to the door and pushing her gently out watched her walk off, muttering. Nothing would happen to her, she was completely in control of her drunkenness.

The Englishman had gone home, but the schoolmaster, already a little drunk, his friend the doctor, Pibourdin, and old Larrau were finishing their belote as he came in, and Larrau called out,

"There you are. I'd begun to think you weren't going to show yourself here."

"Is there any reason why he shouldn't?" Vincent asked irritably.

"None at all," Larrau said. He gave his screeching laugh. "Now he's here I can ask him whether, at last, he agrees with me that children are a curse."

"Shut up," Vincent said.

"I am quite sure," Pibourdin said, smiling finely, "that the first thing I shall hear in purgatory, before I've been in the place five minutes, will be Larrau's terrible laugh."

"Oh, leave him be," Michal said, "he's only saying at the top of his voice what the rest of the village is saying in corners. It's a fact that Philippe is in prison in Grasse."

"I am sorry," Pibourdin said.

Larrau's eyes were sparkling with infantile malice. "Of course you are sorry, we're all sorry, I'm sorry. But I don't like children, and it amuses me when I think of the way old women, and some men, fall on their knees to them, oh the pretty love, the little angel, and then all but one in a million turn out proper rascals. A mistake I never made. There are no rebels or ungrateful sinners in *my* family."

Restraining Vincent by an arm round his neck, Dr. Bertin said amiably,

"Yes, you're a clever fellow, but are you happy?"

"Of course I'm happy! I've had sons and they've done as I told them. What's more, I have never in my life done anyone any

[147]

harm, and never wanted to. I've always avoided doing what would cost me money, and always done exactly what I wanted to do. Anyone who says he believes in benefiting others before himself is a hypocrite. Mind you—" he laughed again—"if he says it to me, and I can take him up on it and get him to do something on the spot that benefits me, I do. Serve him right."

"You're not anything like such a brute as you pretend," the doctor said. "I've even known you put your hand in your pocket for a family in a bad way."

"Never!" Larrau said.

"Yes."

Stretching dangerously the bundle of cords that did duty with him as a neck, Larrau said furiously,

"No, no, it's not true."

"Certainly it hasn't happened more than once—" the doctor began soothingly.

"That's not too bad, in eighty years," Larrau cackled.

"—and you certainly are not a hypocrite. I must say, though, that I'm thankful there are more hypocrites than Larraus in the world. A whole race of Larraus—my God!"

"It might not be soft living," Larrau said, grinning, "but it would be much simpler. No soldiers, no politicians, no clever madmen, everybody minding his own business and taking only what he can get without getting himself killed. There are worse worlds. We live in one of them!"

"Monsieur Michal," Vincent said, with tipsy formality, "you are one of two people in the village for whom I feel liking and respect. If there is any way I can be of use to you, you have only to speak."

"Time you came home, you idiot," Dr. Bertin said.

He lifted the schoolmaster to his feet, found his beret, put it on him, drawing it down to his small delicate ears, and took him away. "I have my car," he told Larrau, who had scrambled up and was making ready to go. "I'll take you as well."

"Thanks. I prefer to die on my feet," Larrau said affably. "The road to my house is no bowling green for drunks."

Michal went back to the bar. After a time he realized that Pibourdin was sitting on alone because there was something he intended to get off his chest. Reluctantly, he went back to the table.

"Will you have a drink?"

"No more, thanks. But sit down a minute," Pibourdin said in a soft voice, extraordinarily gentle and affectionate. "I wanted to tell you something, but not in front of the others."

"What is it?"

"Do sit down."

Sitting at the farther side of the table, Michal waited. Pibourdin leaned forward, to make his voice carry across the two or three feet between them. His expression was one of singular candor.

"Listen, I know you'll have to leave this place. Yesterday I talked to our friend Larrau, and tried to persuade him that he was doing himself a bad turn, as well as the rest of us, by forcing you out of the village to let in a summer visitor. As if there weren't enough of these damned foreigners in the district! He doesn't need the money—nor more land. That I know. But I had no success with him. We cantered through the usual sermon about benefiting yourself before you consider other people, and came out at the other end without my having done a pennorth of good . . . If you have any idea that he might change his mind—"

"I haven't."

"—give it up. He's a stone. But that's not what I wanted to say . . . My brother-in-law, you know, owns hotels in Nice, Menton, Cap Ferrat, not the least profitable hotels on the coast, oh, not by any means. Nothing in the world would give me more pleasure than to arrange for you to go to any one of them as top chef. I should be doing him an enormous service—incalculable —as well as making myself extremely happy. All you need is to tell me which of these places you would like to live in. For myself, I should prefer Cap Ferrat."

His air of kindness, and the delicacy with which he put his

offer, as if the benefit would be all on the side of himself and his brother-in-law, touched Michal in spite of himself. They were, he knew, perfectly genuine.

He knew, too, that no one was more willing to help a man lying flat on his face in the gutter than Alfred Pibourdin. But let the victim of misfortune get on his feet, and begin to prosper, and all the demons of envy, malice, and the suspiciousness of an old woman surrounded by heirs woke in Pibourdin, and although he might not go so far as to try to ruin him again, he did not forgive him, and pursued him with spiteful malice.

For the time being, Pibourdin was all honey and sensitive benevolence. Thank him for them—it is after all pleasant to be encouraged and flattered—and leave it at that, Michal said to himself.

"It's very good of you," he said warmly. "Thank you. If I decide to stay in the south, I'll gladly make use of you. At the moment I haven't made up my mind."

"My dear fellow," Pibourdin cried, "don't talk about leaving this part of the country. You mustn't dream of going away. Think of your friends!"

"Thank you," Michal said again.

He had every intention of considering the offer. He was ready to consider anything. When you are tumbling down a cliff, a cranny full of vipers can be a refuge.

Toward one o'clock, when he put the lights out in the café, he noticed the yellow streak under the door of the bedroom. Does she expect me to spend tonight with her? he thought dryly.

He went downstairs, into Philippe's bedroom. The bed was not made up, and he stretched himself on it as it was, in his clothes. He had endured a great deal during the day, and used up the last grains of even his energy, patience, toughness, he was thankful to lie down anywhere.

He fell asleep at once, and slept calmly and deeply until his usual hour for waking.

13

In the morning he telephoned Gaudo and asked to see him as soon as possible. "Come over now," the Commissioner said, "I have time."

"I should like to see Philippe," Michal went on. There was silence at the other end, and he added shrewdly, "I know that if it can be arranged, if anyone can arrange it, you can."

"Certainly I can arrange it. There are few things I can't arrange—I'm not asked to advise on running the country, it would be run more sensibly if I were—and I can't arrange for you to live to be ninety, but if you want to see Philippe for half an hour this morning you shall have him. Trust me."

When Michal was shown into his room by the squinting constable, Gaudo spread his arms widely. He was in the highest spirits.

"Ah, my friend," he thundered, "you see before you a happy man. Let me tell you about it. When I was a boy of sixteen I decided to be a poet. You know, who doesn't?, what became of that—one volume of poems, tracings of Valéry, Apollinaire,

Cocteau, and the rest. But I am not a fool, and right away I realized that there are quicker and safer ways to becoming a power. And I became what you see me, a big gross man-bull, a provincial minotaur, and a Cicero of eloquence. But I am a persistent fellow, with an enormous appetite, and when I might have been throwing money about, and having women, a great many women, not just one, a little too domesticated, I sat at home and wrote—poems, a novel, plays. The poems and the novel have been destroyed, but this morning I hear that my play, my latest play, the latest of twelve—my Benjamin—has been accepted in Brussels, yes, Brussels. I have friends there. Well, I have friends everywhere, but they are not all useful to me."

"My congratulations," Michal said.

"We shall see, we shall see. And don't imagine that I'm going —at my age—to turn into a professional writer. I told you, I'm not a fool, not romantic. . . . Well, now, what can I do for you? Ask me anything—well, anything I want to do."

"I want information and advice—"

"Oh, advice. I give better advice than anyone in the world, and it costs me nothing. What d'you need?"

Careful to keep out of his voice any emotion, Michal said,

"I take it that there is nothing I can do to save Philippe? I mean—the money he took was mine, if I could have looked forward I'd have preferred to lose it rather than have him arrested—"

Gaudo cut him brusquely short. "You don't, I take it, stretch these fine benevolent sentiments to the other scoundrels?"

"Of course not."

"There is nothing you can do for him," Gaudo said with friendly contempt. "Even if he weren't an accomplice of the two others, he's in trouble in Nice—one of his *respectable old trouts* —an American trout . . . I'm told that in America the trout are the size of tunny . . . He swears she gave him her notecase with fifty thousand francs in it, but she says certainly not, she doesn't pay that highly. She's so furious at being gypped by him that the scandal when the story comes out doesn't frighten her. And, well, there you are, my friend."

He was eying Michal with as much curiosity as good humor. What, he wondered, are his motives for wanting to be quixotic? Not generosity—not only generosity. His vanity? The wish to seem a fine largehearted fellow?

"It's what I expected," Michal said. He did not misunderstand the look in Gaudo's eyes, but he would lose a second fortune rather than satisfy his curiosity. "I should be very much obliged if you would tell me what exactly"—he hesitated—"the position of my wife is in all this."

"Ah." Gaudo wrapped himself in an invisible toga. "Madame Michal must, you'll understand this, be considered as an accessory—at the best. The most innocent. Perhaps she is not involved more than this. Perhaps . . . First, we shall need to see her again—you needn't scowl at me, it will be short, very short, she'll have to sign her statement, since yesterday she was not in a state to sign anything. And perhaps I or Monsieur Garuche may ask her a question—"

Michal interrupted him. "This time not without a lawyer there."

"Oh. You think I was unfair?"

"Not unfair," Michal said, "but a little too much yourself. I should have brought someone, Jouassaint or another fox, to keep an eye on you."

Gaudo did not resent the implied respect for his skill. Smiling broadly, he said,

"Y'know, I felt yesterday that I'd struck bottom in her. She could, I mean, be telling the truth when she says she wasn't in on it from the beginning. Philippe could be lying about that out of conceit, or—more likely—out of sheer indifference—so much else in his head, more exciting, that he forgot exactly what had and hadn't been arranged between them. Y'know, Michal, it's only a very exceptional man or woman who doesn't—in the end —come out with the truth. Most of them, without really think-

[153]

ing about it, believe that the police have occult ways of uncovering lies—and they begin to be afraid it will be worse for them to be caught lying, and so they speak. A fear of this sort isn't one people take lightly, however impudent and determined they are beforehand." His eyes danced. "I daresay it's an instinct left over from our more frankly savage ancestors, with their fear of the local wizard. What d'you say to that?"

"That a lawyer is strictly necessary," Michal said coolly.

Gaudo gave him an almost affectionate glance. "Tell me something, my friend. Do you resent her?"

"Resent?" Michal growled.

He took his time about starting off a cigarette at the lighter Gaudo held out to him in a hand the size and color of a leg of pork.

"It would be natural," Gaudo said.

"After so many years, thirty, of trusting her, and working together, working hard, resentment doesn't enter into it. I'll do what I can to help her through this."

He had spoken in an impersonal voice, as cold and steady as you please. Gaudo did not believe he was cold, and he felt something between tenderness and derision for this solid fellow, whose shrewdness and devilish energy had not saved him from the commonest of mishaps. The forgiving cuckold, he said to himself.

"I don't," he said, "advise you to employ Maître Jouassaint in this—this salvage operation; he hasn't the manner for it. You'd do better to take on the younger Rodier—the younger, mind, not the elder brother: I don't say he's as good a lawyer as his brother, but if there are women on the jury—or for that matter men don't take kindly to a gross eater with poached eyeballs and a stomach he has managed to press into his thighs. To balance matters in the family, the younger has an eighteenth-century profile and a voice he owes, I daresay, to the Italian his father married, not a concert organ but a fine tone. If anybody can convince a jury that Madame Michal is, forgive me, I'm not joking, far from it, an injured repentant woman, he can. What's more, he'll put his soul into it, he believes in women as others believe in preference shares or Our Lady, he's an obdurate romantic. As I might be if I read fewer letters denouncing husbands, wives, neighbors, sisters-in-law, all anonymous. And not, mark you, that they are a hundred percent lies. There are no innocent people."

"When," asked Michal, "do you expect the trial?"

Gaudo pushed forward his fine flexible lip. "That, my friend, has nothing to do with me, it's the business of the Director of Public Prosecutions, Monsieur Denis-Didier Fouchet."

"So you can't do anything about it?"

"Oh, I'll have a word with him," Gaudo said. "He's not the most approachable man in the department, but he'll listen to me. I know him, y'know. We'll try for November, it's just possible—there isn't a great deal pending. Your troubles, in fact, are by way of being a godsend at dinner parties."

"I'll call on the younger Rodier," Michal said.

"Do."

"And I'm much obliged to you for—"

"Nothing, it's nothing. I like to give advice." This was true. "You'll find him sympathetic. And, y'know, the fact that you feel as you do will count—immensely—with any jury. You are willing to stand up in court and say: I have no resentment etc etc?"

Michal was perfectly aware of the contempt a cuckold deserves, and that in the matter of this noble contempt there was nothing to choose between the well-to-do intelligent man facing him and the old woman selling newspapers at the corner of the street outside the Town Hall.

"Yes."

Gaudo leaned forward. "Don't hold it against me," he said warmly, "that I know too much about your affairs. I—well, look at me, you'd say, wouldn't you, that I had never in my life been ashamed or humiliated or even disappointed. You would be quite wrong."

The unfeigned candor of his voice and in his eyes surprised Michal into speaking frankly. He said calmly.

"Yesterday was in fact the worst moment of my life. And, mind you, I'm sixty, I can say completely truthfully that I've had a long run of luck. To have waited until sixty for your bad moment—not many can say as much. And to get it over at sixty, that's not unlucky either. No, I have no complaints."

Gaudo stood up. "We'll have the young sinner in now, shall we?"

14

"**D**on't let my being here annoy you," Gaudo said genially, "and don't think I'm listening to you with more than a quarter of one ear." He settled himself behind his desk and began to examine a file lying on the blotter. "I have plenty to do."

Apart from one leather armchair, its seat worn down at one side to a depth that further disconcerted a timid visitor to this room, there was only the wooden settle. After a second's hesitation, Michal sat down at one end of it. Pointing to the other, he said,

"Sit down, boy, sit down."

As a very young child, Philippe had a habit, carried into his adolescence, of propping his left ankle on his knee and holding it there, with both his slender hands. Seeing him seated like this on the narrow bench, Michal lost a little of the cunning with which he had meant to speak.

"Why did you do it?" he exclaimed.

Had Philippe expected the question? He answered promptly. The half-caressing glance was familiar and an illusion born of the extreme clearness of his pupils, shadowed by thick black eye-lashes as a pond is by reeds.

"I didn't want to cook for the rest of my life."

"Then in God's name why didn't you say so?"

"You never asked me what I wanted to do," Philippe said, smiling. "You made the plans and said what was to happen." In half-confidential tones, he went on, "You know, I meant to disappear quietly, in New York or London, whichever you sent me to. But when this chance came—"

"Chance?"

"Yes, I was a bloody fool, I should have known it was crazy. I was impatient."

No trace, not the faintest, of a feeling that his action had been anything except ill-timed, clumsy. Michal made an effort to grasp the state of mind, the complete absence from it of any sense of remorse. He failed. It was as hopeless as trying to understand a foreign language by watching the speaker's lips.

"Didn't it strike you that what you thought of doing was rather worse than clumsy? That—let's say it was heartless and wicked?"

Philippe stroked his ankle for a moment, frowning lightly. He might have been asking himself whether it was worth while talking.

"Well, you know, dad—what do you *get* in this world by being, as you'd say, well-behaved? I mean, look round you, what are the well-behaved young fellows, who did what their parents wanted, doing with themselves? They're driving streetcars and serving behind counters and teaching thick-eared brats their letters and marrying and bringing up children to serve in shops and the rest of it. Say I'd been born rich, no one would have blamed me for amusing myself—it's the luck of the draw. Come to that—" his voice picked up a thread of mockery—"nobody asked me if I wanted to be born, any more than you asked me if I wanted to be a chef. Or any more than my mother, whoever she was, probably another Rouché, asked me if I would like to

[158]

be dropped at the side of the road like a heavy parcel. I mean, it's absurd, the whole thing is absurd. If you can get what you want, get it—that makes sense. Besides—" he made a gesture of impatience—"oh, it's no good talking to you."

"Didn't you want anything except the life you were living in Nice? The women you got hold of—"

"Of course I did," Philippe interrupted him. "But it did to go on with. In America I'd have done better." The contempt in his voice and glance softened to merriment. "People are the same everywhere, tickle them and they laugh and say: Dear boy, how sweet you are tonight, don't go, stay with me, do stay . . . Pouh!"

Michal felt a prick of anger. "You won't always be irresistible!"

"No, but by then—" Philippe began. He went off into a fit of laughter, the clearest sound in the world. "Oh, dad, oh, dad, how you resent my wanting things you never thought of wanting in the whole of your respectable life of keeping out of trouble, and slaving day in and day out, and being known as a decent reasonably honest man able to pull a modest little string or two if he keeps within bounds, and everyone, even the police, like him. As why shouldn't they? You'll never give any trouble!"

"If you'd told me what it was you wanted," Michal said quietly, "I'd have tried to help you."

"Oh, yeah! If what I wanted was what you thought sensible and respectable and moral. Morality! It stinks, dad, it stinks."

Michal said nothing. Why at this moment, glancing over his shoulder, should he see a road covered with large stones, twisting downward to a walled harbor? It vanished, leaving behind it a feeling of empty hands. With an immense effort he said,

"There are other things—pride, kindness, fidelity . . ."

"For whose sake?"

"Why, for your own."

Philippe looked at him with sincere astonishment. "Dad, you don't, you can't believe that guff. I mean, believe it. You're not, not really a fool." He went on with exasperated contempt, "That's what I can't swallow—the deliberate lying. I mean, some

[159]

people say these things because they're stupid and haven't thought since they were born. You're not stupid, you're even clever."

The grief Michal felt was as frantic as he would have felt if he had been watching the boy drown, unable to move a foot to help him.

"Oh, my God," he groaned, "I can't do anything."

"Don't try," Philippe jeered, "you'll get nowhere."

"Don't you know how proud I was of you?"

"Oh, yeah. *And* jealous."

From grief, such grief, to choking anger is less than a step. Half suffocated, Michal said,

"What the hell d'you mean?"

Philippe smiled. "Of course you were jealous. Old men are always jealous of us, us young. They can't help being . . . Even before you knew about Ti . . ." He had enough grace in him to stammer a little, and go on in a changed voice, almost appealing, "Daft of her to give herself away. I'd never have said anything about it. And you know, dad—"

"I know that whatever happens to you you'll never sink lower," Michal said violently.

Philippe shrugged. "I don't blame you. But don't pretend you're better or sweeter-tempered or nobler than the rest of us."

In the corner of his eye Michal saw Gaudo's fixed on him in a look of pity and the liveliest interest, and checked himself.

"I don't pretend anything," he said. "If I could wipe out that —that particular exploit by thrashing you I should probably do it. And yet," he added sorrowfully, and with a bitter candor, forcing himself to it by an effort of his whole powerful body, "I don't hate you for it, and except when I lose my temper I don't even blame you. Why should I? You're as God made you—even if you don't know yourself."

"If," Philippe said mockingly, "I had an idea in hell what you're talking about!"

A silence. Michal thought: He couldn't be more lost to me if he were dead. Think of it like that. Think: A year, four years ago, Philippe died. . . . Twaddle, sentimental twaddle, he thought dryly, he's alive in front of me, soiled by his own hands, perhaps ruined, and this is the moment I pick on to wipe him out.

He had an extraordinary sensation, as though a fissure opened behind his eyes: the darkness rolling from it cleared and he thought: It's useless to think of loving a handsome affectionate good child who doesn't exist, or being proud of his looks and their effect on people, or of the pleasure of teaching him. As he is now, he has nothing to give me. Can I look at him as he is, coldly, callously, and love that? Perhaps it's not possible, I'm not a patient man.

"My God," he said abruptly, "I'd give both my hands to be chopped off to be able to help you."

Philippe made a defensive movement with his arm. "I don't want you to help me," he said truculently. "You're the last person."

"Well, I'm sorry," Michal said, "You'll have to swallow it, I'm sorry for you, if I could I'd let you off everything and trust to your coming to your senses in a less pedestrian life than I was planning for you. It's out of my hands, you're out of my hands, for the moment I can't do anything for you except tell you that so far as I'm concerned you're in the clear."

For a minute, he thought the young man was going to break down. His face worked as it did when he was eight or nine and confessing to some childish crime. Then, pulling himself together, he said,

"Great scene. But I can't imagine what you're after—what you hope to get out of it. Are you being a Christian, by any chance?"

"No."

"Then what's the score?"

"Damned if I know," Michal said. "But—you're not going to get out of this without spending a certain time in prison, I've no idea how long—when it's over you can . . ." He hesitated, trying to find the phrase least likely to exasperate the young man.

Before he had found it, Philippe burst out laughing. "Oh, that's it! Begin again, eh? Oh, subtle old dad, a stretch of bread and water and the boy'll be thankful to get back to a decent life in the kitchen. That's what you think. Let me tell you something—" leaning forward, his eyes sparkling with amusement, he was for a moment nothing but a young man of the freshest most moving good looks—"I'm never going to give in, never. I know what I'm up against, I always knew it, from the day I began to think, all the swinish dullness, what you call decency— somehow I'm going to keep clear of it, if it kills me, but it won't."

Since I'm not trying to be Christian, Michal thought coldly, and it's not a question of pity, I can wait.

Again, the image of a road invaded his mind, but this time it was a road stretching out of sight across a plain, at night; the moon threw over it the shadows of great stones, shadows of inconceivable depth and blackness. He realized vaguely that this road, like the other, was scored on the floor of his mind, it was very old, perhaps something out of his childhood, or even older than himself. When does a man's life begin and when end? he asked himself. Not at the beginning, not at the end.

He said nothing more, and looked at Gaudo.

Gaudo nodded; he pressed a bell on his desk and when the constable opened the door jerked his head without speaking. He did not open his mouth until the door closed again behind Philippe: then he said,

"My dear fellow, you did what you could. But, you know—*I* know—there's nothing to be done for these youngsters who've made up their minds from the start that society has it in for them just because they're not dull and submissive, not like you and me, not timid greasy canting double-tongued hypocrites. You can't reach them, they prefer *not* to be treated decently—for the good logical reason that it would mean they're not the fine tough rebels they believe they are. D'you see what I mean? Treating that boy generously was like pouring acid on him, he couldn't stand it. If you'd cursed him to hell he'd have known where he was."

"I suppose so," Michal said.

"Don't think I've written him off," Gaudo said with the kindness he allowed himself when he felt, as he did now, immeasurably superior in worldly experience and acumen to the man he was talking to. "He can still, when he comes out, have the luck to see through his delusions about himself. With that face, it's unlikely, but . . ."

With his gross hand, he sketched a gesture of a certain delicacy.

Michal stood up. "Thanks."

"Oh, by the way. Yesterday, when he was told he had the right to nominate a lawyer, or have one assigned to him, he said: Assign anybody you like, it's all the same to me. . . . Unless you object, I propose to get my nephew assigned to him, he's a young fellow, not thirty-five, and conscientious and sensible. He'll do as much as he can."

"What's his name?"

"Maître Joseph—my sister's son. I can't assign him, but I can move my elbow."

Outside, in the brilliant light, and the heat, he felt as cold as a stone, and as lifeless. Life came back to him when he was crossing the cobbled square to his car. I have only to hang on, he thought, all isn't lost yet: beginning and end are separated by a long enough road for anything to happen.

He was unhappy, but he noticed with acute pleasure the contrast between a young woman's white arm and the three long sticks of well-baked bread she was carrying. He had come out without his breakfast of bread-rolls and coffee: he stopped the car at the little bakery she must have been into, and bought himself a long thin stick, hard and slightly warm, and ate it ravenously as he drove away.

15

He found Lotte where she ought to be, and where he expected to find her, in the kitchen, standing beside young Truchi, watching critically his awkward fingers at work stuffing a small bird. During the next few hours, he made time to look at her now and then, stealthily. A body which had kept its firmness for so many years was not likely to lose its resilience in a day: under the thin blouse clinging damply to her skin, the movement of her back was as quick as ever; for all the heaviness of her long thighs she was as supple as a young woman. What, in the past few weeks, had aged, was her face: the cheekbones were more prominent, and below them the flesh had been pressed by a thumb into two hollows stretching to the line of her jaw which, it too, had hardened and become more noticeable.

None of this gave him any feeling of satisfaction.

Lunch over, he said,

"Come into the bedroom, I want to talk to you."

He had meant to tell her about his talk with Philippe, but found that he could not—no more than he had been able to question Philippe about her. The mere notion revolted him. All he could do was to repeat part of what Gaudo had said, and warn her.

"When you go there to sign your statement, you'll be questioned again—probably not a great deal. But this time a lawyer will go with you, the lawyer"—he hesitated—"who will defend you at the trial. And he'll arrange now whatever has to be arranged, I know very little about these things, so that you are free—can stay here, I mean—until then." He looked her in the face, with an expression of friendly irony. "I need you here."

"What will they ask me?"

"What do you think? Whether you did or didn't know, beforehand, what was being planned. I doubt whether Gaudo believes you."

She faced him. "Do you?"

"Would you be surprised if I told you I didn't?" he said dryly.

"No. Not, not surprised. Only—" her voice was far from being calm, but it was controlled and steady—"I don't know what to say to convince you. Ask me—oh, anything you want to ask."

If, he thought, there were some way of running a fingernail round the inside of your mind to collect the truth, like scraping a casserole.

"You told them you didn't know what was in Philippe's mind about the money. Is it true? Or was the whole thing, breaking into this room, manhandling you, tying you to the bed, a put-up job, a farce? No, don't answer quickly. . . . I know, I tell you I know, I understand that scruples—gratitude and all that—kindness—don't come into it when it's a question of—of happiness. But if you have any honesty or kindness left, tell me the truth. I can stand the truth. What I can't stand, what makes me want to kill, is being lied to." He added with calm cruelty, "You can understand that."

"I told the truth," she said.

"You were taken by surprise when they came in here?"

"Yes."

[165]

"You didn't expect it, but—after it had happened—you encouraged Philippe to go ahead with his plans to ruin me and make a laughingstock of me?"

"Yes, yes—"

"So why should I believe anything you tell me?"

"Because . . . why should I want to keep this one shred of lies?" she said feverishly. "I'm telling you the truth, he didn't tell me beforehand—I agreed to it *after* . . ."

"When did you decide to go away with him?"

She moved her arms in the curving gesture of a woman lifting a heavy child. "Afterwards. After the robbery, when I knew he was going. Before that—" she hesitated—"before that there was no need, I had him with me."

He felt a stab of rage and contempt—and jealousy. "What was it in him that made you . . . why did you fall for him?"

He noticed the change in her voice when she talked about Philippe; it had become deep and harsh, almost raucous, a purely visceral sound: he found it almost unbearable.

"He was so alive—y'know, violently alive. And careless and amusing."

Perhaps all women, he thought, are anarchists and crave violence, and all, in their secret hearts, want to be given over to something dangerous, unmanageable, unsafe. In that way she was as little moral, as little held back by scruples, as Philippe himself. Like him, she went directly for what she wanted. And like him, she would have asked, sincerely—with infinitely more sincerity than malice: Why not? What is more important than happiness? . . . I've neglected her a little, he thought dryly, in these last years, sexually and in other ways; this was a—a convulsion of her strong body, a kind of animal egotism. She was scarcely responsible.

At the same time with these half-tolerant half-brutal reflections he had a horrible sensation of having been laid open; it is never less than comically humiliating to lose at one blow all your comfortable self-deceptions and illusions. What his mind, with an effort, could accept his body rejected violently, as violently as it rejected the supreme insult of pity.

"I've spoiled everything for you," she said under her breath.

He shook his head. "You couldn't do that. Not quite everything. You've done some damage, of course, no one enjoys being tricked, and when it's with your own—no, no, he isn't my son." He laughed shortly. "It takes some tearing out, by God."

"For me everything is spoiled—and I'm too old to forgive myself."

Ah, he thought, without cynicism, what you mean is: I'm not young enough now to hold any man for long, least of all a young man.

"You're still attractive," he said coolly, "you've worn remarkably well, you know."

To his surprise, this made her laugh, a sound between mockery and genuine amusement. Impulsively, she moved toward him, a movement she checked with a savage jerk of her body on the strong muscles of her waist.

"Do you believe I didn't plan to take the money?"

He said, "Yes"—out of indifference and a half-contemptuous regret.

I shall never be certain, he thought calmly, never absolutely sure. . . . But even if she is lying—what can you do with a half-childish half-lawless creature except punish or forgive her? . . . She was not heartless, not corrupt: what had happened to her might happen as easily to any immature human being, with simple strong greeds, which got itself trapped in the twists of an affair begun, thoughtlessly, between two little animals. Once in it, she had to go on to the end. Her last act, when she helped Philippe to ruin him, was as natural and inevitable as all the rest. After all, he thought, what is she but a completely natural sensual woman?

He had the wry honesty to admit to himself that—for some time now—she had meant less to him than his "son." And therefore had robbed him of less. And therefore was infinitely easier to make sense of—and to pity—with more than a touch of contempt.

He turned to leave her. As he reached the door she spoke in her ordinary clear full voice.

"Shall I make up the bed in Philippe's room?"

If she had spoken humbly he would not have felt this lift of the heart. "Is that what you want?"

"No."

"Very well," he answered, "leave things as they are."

16

Two or three weeks later, in mid-June, he heard, through Maître Jouassaint, that the Parisian who was buying the Hotel Moderne Aristide did not want to make use of it before next spring: he was willing to buy it at once and leave it empty for several months. On the same day, Gaudo, dining in the restaurant, told him casually that he could count on the trial coming off in November, possibly in the first week.

I've been given a reprieve, he thought. Not a long one but long enough to enjoy.

His spirits rose crazily, he decided to try to keep the restaurant going until November, and next day he asked the schoolmaster to find out for him whether Larrau would let him stay on for six months, from the end of his lease.

The answer Larrau made was ambiguous, but not a flat No, and Vincent invited them to his office in the mairie to talk about it.

"He won't come," Michal said.

"Oh, he'll come," Vincent said, smiling and coughing. "You,

the whole lot of you, misunderstand the old devil, he pretends to detest his fellow men, when in fact what he is is a ferociously nimble-minded egotist; he likes to hear himself talk, and a chance to make malicious remarks to your face—he gets no pleasure out of making them behind your back—is one he won't lose."

He was right. Arriving in the greatest good humor—given that his humor was that of a nimble egotist—Larrau agreed almost without argument to keep the hotel in his own hands for another six months. The lawyers, "sharks in collars," could busy themselves making sure of touching the Parisian's money in January, and there was no need to pay them for arranging a little affair of six months' rent.

"Monsieur Vincent here can make a note of it," he said, "it's his job to make notes. And you'll pay me in advance, plus ten percent for the trouble you're giving me."

"What trouble, in God's name?" asked Michal.

"The anxiety of waiting another half year for my money. Why, I might die!"

"People like you don't die," Michal said calmly, "you've no flesh to lose, and your only passion is for getting your own way —you'll live miserably forever."

Larrau bounced about on his chair in an access of atrocious gaiety and good temper. "Much you know about me. I may be as thin as a horsefly, but horseflies live very well, y'know, very economically and happily."

"Is it your idea of happiness?"

"Why not? It's as good as the next man's," Larrau said, toothless black gums stretched in a wide smile, almost infantile. "Look where yours has led you—to near bankruptcy, done out of your money by your nearest and dearest. I could live without most things, without a family to keep in its place, without—at long last—a woman, without friends, without priests, without eating more than my own cheese and drinking a glass of water, but I couldn't endure being without my own land under my feet, and money to fatten it. If I knew of a way to inject it into myself I'd do it, and go on absorbing it to the last farthing's worth."

Michal laughed. His rich laughter was as much instinct with him as breathing. Even his humiliation did not silence it. Not that his present poverty humiliated him, not in the least, not for an instant. The loss of his savings angered him, and the loss of his jewel of a restaurant, but neither of these losses was a humiliation. What made him grind his teeth secretly was the thought that he had been overreached, that people knew he had been overreached. His shrewdness and naïve vanity joined forces in him to make him see with horrible distinctness what old Larrau—not only Larrau—saw when he looked at the great Aristide Michal: a fine figure of a dupe, the luckless victim of two people he had picked, neither more nor less out of the gutter, and boasted about and cherished. He could avoid—for most of the time—thinking about his "son": this other bitterness, quite as near the bone, woke with him in the morning and walked about the village at his elbow, and even nudged him in the restaurant and the café whenever the Englishman or the doctor or Blaise Vincent steered the conversation adroitly round a dangerous corner, or when he caught Pibourdin's eye resting on him with sly tenderness.

The only man with whom he always felt easy was Paul Larrau. With Larrau he could be certain of meeting neither pity nor a tactful silence. Whenever the old fellow saw a chance to make a spiteful joke at anyone's expense he seized it, no matter the victim or the occasion: it was his greatest pleasure in life, and didn't cost him a penny. Michal's misfortune was a gift to him.

His joyful malice neither embarrassed nor irritated Michal as did the others' tact.

"If it hadn't been for your passion for handling things," he said easily, "I should have left my money in the bank, it would have passed from my possession into yours without either of us

[171]

touching it, and none of this would have happened."

"No, no," Larrau retorted, "you can't blame me. In the first place, you had no need to bring it home. In the second, who asked you to leave it there for a week while you posed as a noble fellow with the Clozel woman? Not I."

"I have something to tell you about that," Vincent exclaimed.

"Later, later."

"It's true. I could have left my money where it was," Michal said lightly. "That piece of idiocy I regret. The other—no. It would be on my conscience."

"Much good your conscience will do you when you're forced to thank Monsieur Alfred Pibourdin for a job!"

"Are you going to take his offer?" asked Vincent.

"I haven't decided."

"It won't, at your age, be pleasant to have to take orders again," Larrau said slyly.

Michal's smile completely hid his rage and bitterness. "Do you believe that anybody will come into a kitchen where *I* am working, to give me orders? I'm not made like that. I work as I please, and if it pleases other people, well and good. If it doesn't, or if I feel like putting on my jacket and walking away, what's to prevent me? So long as I have the energy, I'm free. And, believe me, I have energy for ten lives like mine." He turned to Vincent, and said in the same overbearing voice, "You should begin thinking about your next deputy mayor, my friend. Do you want my advice?"

"You're not going to resign yet?" Vincent said. Surprise and dismay rose in his throat, choking him, and he coughed himself blue in the face. The fit over, he said imploringly, "Not sooner than you must, my dear fellow!"

"At once," Michal said coldly.

Larrau was turning his shrunken gargoyle of a face from one to the other, delighted to be the bearer of a piece of disturbing news. "I can tell you something," he said to Vincent. "Unless you're very quick or very much cleverer than I think you are, you'll find that your new deputy mayor has got more lines out already than you can handle. I mean our friend Pibourdin. If you didn't know that his ambitions go beyond counting barrels of wine and escaping twice a month from his pest of a wife, you know nothing. It's more than ten years since the end of the war, and his little faults and lapses during it have been forgotten—quite rightly. Why shouldn't he have taken pains to survive? Now he wants to be admired and he wants to meddle. Meddling in a small way here, in a village, won't content him for long, but it's a start, and—well, you'll see!"

"He wouldn't be a bad choice," Michal said, "a clever active adroit man, who'll act in our—I mean your—interests to build up his own reputation . . . no, it's not a bad prospect."

Vincent groaned. "I can't bear it."

"There have been occasions—you may remember—when you couldn't bear me."

"My dear fellow, it's the difference between a human being and a monster. You are a politician, and you sometimes get into an intrigue—not for your own benefit—to benefit some deserving or undeserving victim. He's an intriguer, a born intriguer, he intrigues for the pleasure of it, without reason or cause, it will be like having a flea loose in one's shirt. Oh, my God, my God."

Michal roared with laughter. "Your trouble, thank heaven, not mine. . . . What were you going to tell us about Madeleine Clozel?"

Head in his two hands, Vincent said,

"What have I done to deserve my life?"

"Only get yourself born."

"Pibourdin! God help me . . ." He straightened himself. "It wasn't about her. About her boy. I don't think there's anything we can do, but . . . Yesterday I had nothing to do over here, and I stayed in the school for half an hour or so after four o'clock. When I came out there was a group of the older boys in one corner of the yard, the girls and younger boys had gone—very often my little Marthe stays behind for a few minutes, talking—as like as not talking to him—but she was indoors looking after her aunt, who has a colic or something of the sort. . . . I couldn't see anything, but I had a sudden feeling that something very unpleasant was going on: I walked across the yard, and as I got near it the group broke up, most of the lads made off at a run, and the few who didn't stood back, except for two who were offering to help young Clozel dust himself off. He was in an ugly state, blood trickling from the side of his mouth. He had just fended off his two would-be helpers. 'Don't touch me, you,' he said. I let the lot clear off, thinking I could deal with them in the morning—and that I should be able to handle him better alone." He laughed shortly. "I could handle him! He looked at me as if I were made of the same dung as his tormentors, and told me to leave it alone. Not simply leave *him* alone—keep out of the whole affair, take my nose out of it. I was going to take him into the house and wash the blood and dirt off his face—one side looked as if he'd been dragged over the ground. He said, 'Thanks, I don't need help.' And walked off. This morning I questioned him in front of the class; he glared at me in his stony way and said, 'I'm sorry, I don't know what you mean—nothing happened yesterday.' . . . Not a peep out of the class. . . . He wasn't protecting them, you understand. It was pure contempt—or he was only anxious to be left alone—or I don't know . . ."

"What did you do?" Michal asked.

"Nothing. I dropped it. That's why I'm telling you. Did I or didn't I do the right thing? What ought I to have done?"

Larrau said mockingly,

"What did I tell you? If you knew as much about children as I know—and you should, you've had opportunities enough—you'd know they enjoy lying and torturing and destroying. In any case, the boy's no better than a German. Why bring him here? Trust a woman to make trouble, she should have left him where he belonged."

"No, you can't let it go on," Michal said.

Vincent rubbed his hand over his eyes as if to wipe off an image. "My impression is, it won't happen again. It may have been a—what do I mean?—a crisis. And now that the abscess has burst . . . They may be feeling appeased—or ashamed."

"Ashamed of enjoying themselves?" Larrau said. He laughed.

"One of them ashamed," Vincent said, wincing, "the rest appeased or scared."

"That's a pretty low percentage of decency," Michal said dryly.

"My God, one in fifteen! It's abnormally high. How many adult mobs do you suppose are as innocent?"

"In a few years' time those boys of yours are going to form, what d'y'call it?, the community," Larrau said. "I tell you, the only way to live in it is to want nothing you can't reach with your own hands, and to trust no one. I knew in my cradle that there are two sorts of people, those you can make use of and those you can't, and I've never been taken in in my life. A good lesson for you, Monsieur Michal!"

Before Michal could answer, the light sound of a child's footsteps in the stone-tiled corridor brought a look of foolish fond love over the schoolmaster's face. The door of his office opened, and Marthe put her head inside. All three men smiled at her—even Larrau. It was impossible to look at her round face without pleasure; everything about it was sound and placid; only to see it reconciled you to all the most decried virtues in the world: simplicity, modesty, fidelity. Yet she was not a beauty, scarcely even pretty.

"You told me to tell you when the doctor came to look at Aunt Agathe," she said in her light little voice, "he's there now."

"Thank you," her father said with relief, "I'll come, I'll come."

17

In a sense the schoolmaster had been right when he saw the scene in the courtyard as a crisis. The first month or so after Jean Clozel came to the school had served the boys of his age as a sort of apprenticeship in the uses and delights of torture—on a puerile scale, of course, with none of the refinements of adult intelligence and science. But intelligence began to creep in, and suggest ways in which simple roughness and rudeness could be improved on.

When, after he had shaken off the prying headmaster, Jean got home, he found the house empty and remembered, with intense relief, that this was a day in the week when his mother walked three miles to a small château, to do the mending for a large English family. His meal was set ready for him in the kitchen, milk, cheese, a saucerful of wild strawberries, an egg he had only to boil. Without glancing at it, he walked over to the small glass on the dresser, and examined himself with a pretense, very necessary to him, of great coolness. One cheek, the right, had a pattern of deep blackened scratches as if a rake

[176]

had passed over it, where it had been pressed into the gravel. A little fresh blood, since he wiped it, had trickled from his mouth. In forcing a rough piece of wood between his teeth, to make him speak—he had been ordered to repeat a lewd home-made verse about German women—they had torn his tongue and the flesh inside his cheeks. Afraid that they might have broken a tooth, he felt each one in turn with fingers that shook in spite of him, then took his shoes off to see what sort of state his feet were in. At the moment the headmaster came out of the school and started to cross the courtyard they had just forced his shoes back on them after two boys had stamped on each for several minutes with a great deal of skill and application—to teach him, they said smiling, to wear the kind of shoes they all wore.

I should soak these off, he said to himself, looking at his socks. Instead, he set his teeth and dragged at them and was very nearly sick. But the toes, he saw, were not seriously damaged; every nail was black, with blood oozing round the edges, but none were torn off.

Good, he thought carefully.

The damage that hit him hardest was to his clothes. Using a knife, they had cut the jacket in several places, up and across, so that little flaps of cloth hung down.

"My good jacket," he murmured. His lips trembled.

Turning from the glass, he looked at the table for a moment, then broke off a corner of bread and tried to eat it. He couldn't, and had to spit it out. It was less the difficulty of using his torn swollen tongue than his throat, which closed as soon as he asked it to swallow the morsel.

Like his tormentors, he had been making discoveries during the past months. About them and about himself. About himself he had learned that pain, at least when it is no more severe than the pain of a rasped tongue and crushed nails, is less hard to bear than being helpless. It was his helplessness in their hands that was killing him.

About the others he had learned an odd thing. That the least softhearted child—if the words are not a contradiction in terms —is not without his impulses to kindness. And perhaps he despised a little more those boys who, when no one was looking, were friendly to him, even gay.

He sat down, pushing his plate aside, and propping his head between his hands gave himself up avidly to the dream.

By now it was so closely woven, so familiar, that he could enter it at any point, no need to start at the beginning. From the place on the edge of the upper village where the bus to Grasse started, he had worked out a way of reaching Marseilles which did not involve him in using any main road or crossing through any large town. Once in Marseilles he would find a small cargo boat, a German one naturally, in need of a strong young deck hand, which would take him, not directly to Germany, but to Africa, thus throwing pursuers off his track. From Africa, another German ship, on its way to Hamburg, and also short of a deck hand or steward or stoker, would land him near enough home to be able to walk there in a matter of days. At this point the dream ended and a delicious vertigo took its place. But then he had only to go back, verify a bus route, check the bridges over a stream, remind himself of the names of streets in Marseilles leading to the docks—conned over and over again in the maps borrowed from Monsieur Michal on the excuse of pre-paring an essay—and an hour had slipped past, two hours, of complete happiness.

He was not an idiot. In a corner of his mind he knew that his carefully made plan was an impossibility. Dreaming about it in full daylight, or even at night before he fell asleep, was a way of stupefying oneself, like a man drinking too much. Young as he was, he actually knew this.

There were even days when he had the courage to refuse.

This evening—for no reason—as he was walking along the wharf toward the German ship with its single funnel, its flag, and at the head of its gangway the figure of the officer who would not even inquire his age before signing him on, he began to cry.

For no reason.

He cried silently, tears running over his face, between the fingers of the hands he pressed over it. Not a sound, not the least whimper, from a despair without beginning and without end, such despair as only a child, with its new senses, feels.

A faint click—his mother's fingers on the latch of the door into the outer room, her room. His tears stopped. He wiped his face swiftly, wiping with the same gesture the traces of blood round his mouth.

She came into the kitchen very slowly, carrying, as she always did from this particular house, a heavy bundle of linen and children's dresses, and laid it down. He had his face turned from her, and the first thing she noticed was the table.

"Why, Jean, you haven't touched anything! Didn't you like it?"

"Thank you, I wasn't hungry," he said calmly.

She came round in front of him, saw his cheek, and said under her breath, "Ah!", pressing her clenched hand on her mouth.

Without saying another word, she poured a little water into a basin she set down on the table and wringing a handkerchief out in it tried to sponge the deep scratches.

Putting her hand away, gently enough, the boy said, "No, let me."

He took basin and handkerchief over to the dresser, to the small looking-glass, and keeping his back to her cleansed his face thoroughly and slowly; he was putting off the moment when he would be forced to turn round and she would begin questioning him. She spoke behind his back.

"Who did it?"

"No one. Myself. I fell on the gravel."

He turned. In this small room, there was so little space between table and dresser that she had not noticed his bare feet.

Now she saw them. Her face lost what color it had, but she steadied her voice to say,

"You never told me anything about this."

"Why should I?"

"Has—has it been going on long?"

"What are you talking about?" he said coldly. "I'm all right."

There was an iron pan at the side of the stove, half full of lukewarm water. Carrying it with some difficulty to the low cane-seated chair she had once told him was a "nursing chair" that had been her mother's, she put it down on the floor and said,

"Sit here, I'll wash them."

"Certainly not," he answered, "I'll wash them myself."

She stood still and looked at him searchingly, as though she were trying with all the strength of her mind and body to force another face to come from behind his. This look of hers made him uneasy, and when she said, very slowly, "Listen, Jean. I'll make a bargain with you. Let me wash your poor hurt feet and I won't ask any more questions," he agreed quickly, only to escape it.

"Very well—but mind you don't."

Kneeling in front of him, she washed both feet in silence, very gently, glancing up now and then to see whether she were making him wince. Not until she was holding the second foot in her palm and was drying it carefully did she lose hold of herself. Then she said desperately,

"I *must* know."

He took the towel out of her hand. "You promised not to ask questions. Don't promises mean anything to you?"

To his astonishment, she smiled at him with frank gaiety. "You said that like your father."

He did not answer, he never answered her when she said anything about the past, hers: he would not let himself be drawn into it, not by so much as an eyelash.

[180]

"Since you can't eat, I'll make some coffee."

When she was making it she said in a strange distant voice, as if speaking to herself,

"Perhaps after all I did wrong to bring you here. I don't know what to do . . . I could talk to Monsieur Leighton . . ."

A great flame of hope rushed through him and vanished as if the ground had swallowed it. No, they'll never let me go back, he thought. There was the finality of a little death in this thought—death of a bird in the winter, perhaps. He saw her look round the kitchen and before he could stop himself thought: She would be alone here again. He remembered her saying in a calm voice about the people in the village: Some of them *too* would rather I had died in the camp . . . Instinctively he drew back.

"Don't talk about it to anybody," he said coldly. "Things won't be so bad any more."

"How do you know that?"

How did he know it? "They'll be afraid." In a carefully negligent voice he added, "This time they didn't really like it. Two of them didn't."

Standing by the stove, on which she had put a little fresh wood, "for pleasure, not warmth," he held the thick white bowl of coffee between his hands, and drank from it: an extraordinary feeling of ease and suppleness passed into all his limbs.

"This is good," he murmured.

She flashed him a look of gratitude from eyes still young at the bottom of their discolored pits. "When I was a child, my father—he was still the headmaster here then, he had lost a leg and an arm in the war—it vexed him because he used to adore climbing and walking—well, it was he who taught me to make coffee, my mother took very little interest in anything to do with her kitchen, and what my father liked better than anything in the world was to sit out in the sun, in the garden of the schoolhouse—it had carnations and roses then, not herbs— with two bowls of coffee, one for him, one for me, his crutch

leaning against the bench between us, and read aloud. He read
—of course—*Lettres de mon moulin,* but he read as well a
novel called *Vanity Fair* by an English writer, and all La
Fontaine, and, yes, *Candide,* and when my mother scolded him
and said that such a book wasn't suitable for a child he laughed
at her and said: Why do you want to hide from her that there
are other things in the world as well as bowls of coffee and
roses?"

"How old were you?"

"A year younger than you are—eleven."

At this moment she noticed his jacket; he had hung it on the
back of a chair and her eye was caught by the rent in a sleeve.
When, holding it up, she saw the other tears, eight or nine of
them, she said queerly,

"Are you going to tell me these happened when you fell?"

"No."

She looked closely. "They were done with a sharp knife."

"Yes."

For a minute she did not speak. He had brought three suits
with him from Germany, they were all very well made and
very urban, and after one unhappy attempt to persuade him to
wear something more suitable for a French village she did not
dare to speak about it again. Glancing at him furtively, she saw
the effort he was making not to cry. They're his idea of safety,
they're the good solid German life he had, she thought: oh, my
baby, my poor baby.

"I can repair it," she said in a light voice. "You won't be able
to see where it was torn."

"Are you—are you sure?"

She smiled. "Of course I'm sure. Wear one of the others
tomorrow, and when you come home you'll find this one as
good as new. I can do part tonight."

"Thank you very much," he said formally.

"It's very good cloth," she said after a moment, fingering it.
She spoke in a poor humble voice, which scandalized him.

Why does she mind that it's better cloth than any they have here? he thought sharply. He half knew why.

"It's strong," he said. He laughed briefly, in his throat. "They had to work at it to cut it."

"Oh! Jean," she said inaudibly.

"It doesn't matter—since you can mend it."

"As good as new. I promise."

She folded the jacket, and laid it on the bundle of garments she had brought home. Almost for the first time, he noticed how thin were the shoulders supporting her head and small pointed face with its skin like cracked porcelain and colorless mouth. I should do something to help her, he thought swiftly; I could arrange to call at houses for these bundles . . . The thought of carrying them through the village displeased him, and he bit his lip.

When she turned to him and smiled, he had all he could do to keep back words that would have given away his sudden feeling that he was responsible for her in some way. More than that—a sort of warmth.

"You work too hard," he said.

"Oh, no." A little color came into her cheeks. "It's only that I'm untrained, I'm no good for anything but the kind of thing I do. I married too early—seventeen—to do any of the things my father expected. Poor man, he was very disappointed." She went on with a rush. "We might read aloud sometimes . . ."

He drew back instantly, and looked at her as if what she had said was unforgivable.

"I shall go to bed," he said, getting up.

He went without looking at her again.

In his room he stood for several minutes in a stupor of disgust with himself. If *she* had seen and heard me, he thought, his face burning . . . He saw her near him, her large soft arms and placid eyes looking at him with reproach and grief. So it hasn't taken you more than four months to forget me . . . He flung himself on the bed. I haven't forgotten you, he told her desperately, I promise you I haven't, it was a mistake, it was all a horrible mistake, I'm your good Joachim, I haven't forgotten.

The weight of guilt on his heart was completely unbearable. He tried, pressing his face in the pillow, to shut out the image of himself smiling and talking to the woman downstairs, softening toward her, letting her think he was interested in what she said. What happened to me? he thought wildly. I can't bear myself, what sort of beast am I, what can I do now, oh God, what can I do?—this is the end of everything, the end, yes, the very end. *What can I do?*

I can kill myself, he thought.

A heavenly peace and exhaustion spread through his body. He managed to pull his few clothes off before falling asleep, the soundest sleep, sweet, dreamless, he had ever known in this room.

18

At this very moment yellowed bony fingers were ripping open a letter which had been lying about for several hours. Glancing at it when Ahmed brought it in and laid it on the writing table, Leighton had seen from the envelope that it came from his solicitor, and he knew what it contained, a list of securities he had asked the fellow to send him. It was of little interest, and could wait. Nowadays he was curiously reluctant to read anything that came to him from the world outside this corner of Provence in which, like an old hare lying in its burrow with legs drawn up into its belly, he waited.

The sheet he drew out was not a list of securities, it was a personal letter to tell him, "since I believe you no longer see the English newspapers," that his ex-wife had died, suddenly, in London, the evening before the letter had been written.

His heart began to beat heavily, as though with each movement it were pushing aside a weight of blood. He had an extraordinary sensation of darkness, inside and outside himself, darkness and nothing else, a total absence, a desert in which were no sounds, scents, shadows, or flickering lights, or things breathing.

He came out of it to find himself in the room where he had spent so much time writing, a few lines at a time, the story of his marriage to the dead woman. The manuscript was still in a drawer of the table; he meant to have it copied before he sent it away to his solicitor with the instructions for publishing it after his own death, and he was waiting to drive into Nice and ask advice from the English consul about a reliable typist. Taking it out of the drawer, he began turning the pages. A familiar excitement, cruel and very pleasant, seized him. No excitement known to human beings, neither danger nor gratified ambition nor cruelty itself nor sex, is as acute, as deeply satisfying, as the excitement of bringing off a new truthful stroke of art—and this he had done. He knew it in the only way a man—writer, painter, musician—can know these things, with the marrow of his brain. Some energy and potency had left him, to lodge in the work; this book was not so many dead phrases, it now lived in a mysterious dimension of its own and could reach out from it to touch other lives. In it he had done, he *knew,* what Strindberg and lesser men failed to do because blinded by their fear or anger; he had stripped to the bone, to the naked enduring unforgiving bone, the enmity between male and female, at its sharpest in their sex play. His years of patient brooding on it had created an image as clear, cold, and glittering as ice. Some people—and not only the woman for whose eyes he had written it—might find it indecent and insupportable, but it was genuine. A truthful image of the human condition, as true in its narrow small way as the *Iliad* or *Lear*.

"So why," he said aloud, "should I mind dying?"

He heard his servant move very quietly in the room next this. He knew what would happen now, the door would open, noiselessly, a crack, just wide enough for an eye to look into the room and see that he was all right. He waited. The door opened without a sound, the eye appeared, withdrew, the door closed, and he could go back to caressing the pages under his hand.

He was not reading them. But a phrase which suddenly caught his eye made him realize the danger he was running. Too late.

Too late. She came into the room, and he watched her walk across it, half laughing, letting the crimson cloak slip from young bare shoulders. He had taken her to Covent Garden to hear *Electra*, it was the first time she had been there and she was still quivering with happiness, her eyes dark with excitement, her unpainted lips a clear red like the cloak he had given her for the occasion. "Oh, the heavenly heavenly evening," she said, smiling. She touched his face with a light finger. . . . The sudden violent memory flooded him with a passion he had not felt at the time, far more piercing than anything he could have felt then. And now a score of such moments pricked him, falling on his dry skin like spring rain. Nothing about her was more wonderful than her quickness to enjoy things—she had kept alive into adult life a child who saw them as if seeing them for the first time, with a treasure of surprise and delight. This was what made people open their arms to her. It was the miraculous gift she gave them from her excess of aliveness and gaiety. And to me, he thought.

He remembered another moment, in the country near Milan, when, with two other young women and their husbands she had been bathing in a deep stream running through a marsh. When a snake, a long vigorously moving snake, crossed suddenly from one side to the other, its little head brushing the surface of the water, the others scattered in panic, with little screams: only she stood quietly, up to her smooth finely muscled thighs in the clear stream, watching its swift passage, her lips parted in a joyous smile. "Did you see it?" she called to him. "It moved like this," and she used her arms in a gesture so childish and supple that it brought grief into his throat.

Ahmed came in again, this time to light the oil lamps. He lit them and waited. Since, this evening, his master had not wanted to make the effort to go to the hotel and had dined at home on goat cheese, bread, cherries and a carafe of Bellet, he might want something before he went to bed.

"Nothing," Leighton said impatiently, "I don't want anything. I'll call you when I need helping upstairs."

Alone again, he thought: That delight she took in things she could see and touch was her life, and that life was peculiarly strong in her: if there is any existence after death—he did not believe there is, but like most passionate and passionately repressed natures, he played with the thought—she must be saying what Achilles said—*Would that I were a slave on earth, bound to some poor man who has a hard struggle to keep life in him. Even like that it is better to be alive than . . .* and the rest of it.

His thoughts drifted. If we can't satisfy the demands life makes on us, it will punish us. At what moment did I flinch aside—and deserve the rest of my empty life?

In a passage of his book he had spoken of her as having the instincts of a not very highly developed animal, "from which," he wrote, "it follows that to speak of her disloyalty and mean lies as a crime is as meaningless as accusing a hyena for killing a sick or wounded beast." Now, abruptly, as if a film had been torn from his eyeballs, he thought: But I didn't see far enough: the fact is that, behind any act, of any man or woman, there is always some desperate need, a fear of losing some good or a hope long dreamed of and suddenly seen within reach. I was in her way . . .

He got up and went to a window. They were all still open —it was after eleven, but not wholly dark, a bluish half-light, and usually about now one or more nightingales began their soliloquies or choirs in the trees sheltered from the north by the house itself. Tonight there was only one singer, but it let itself go with enough energy to defeat any rival, had there been one, drawing the night to itself to give it back in pure heartless notes and trills prolonged almost beyond bearing . . .

> *Sile philomena*
> *pro tempore* . . .

But he had forgotten how it went on, and only remembered English words that might or might not be a translation—*keep quiet to let the heart cry out.*

"Ahmed," he called, and when his servant came in said, "Shut the windows to keep out that horrible row. . . . All right, all right, that will do, go away, I don't want you yet."

He went back to his writing table and the manuscript scattered across it. I can publish it at once, he thought calmly. Since I can't destroy her living—this is twice she's cheated me, the little whore—I can destroy her ghost, the charming image she has left in all their minds. Not what I planned, but better than nothing.

For a moment, as if looking over his shoulder, he saw the blackened ruins of his life. You yourself destroyed it, he thought. How ridiculous that you didn't notice what you were doing. Now there is no more time.

In the warm room, where even the old wood of his table kept a little of the heat of the long burning day, he shivered a little. Have I the energy to tear it up now, tonight, he asked himself, or shall I tell Ahmed to do it?

Half smiling at the absurdity, he thought: It shouldn't be destroyed by a servant.

It took him quite a time to crumple each page into a ball, not too tightly, for easier burning. The stove, an elaborate affair of iron and tiles, emptied at the end of April, had been left empty. He filled it with the two hundred-odd pages of his very fine very legible writing, set a match to them, and watched them burn. When there was only ash, he opened a window again.

He felt no emotion, neither regret for what he had just done

[189]

nor any feeling of satisfaction—nothing.

Outside, in the half-darkness, there was only silence, warmth, and the pain of his solitude, a naked longing and grief.

"This night, this heart," he said.

He felt a burning thirst, his tongue and throat both parched, and when Ahmed brought him in the pitcher and a glass he thought that he had never in his life tasted colder sweeter water.

"Now you can help me to bed," he said gently.

19

Had he been less absorbed in himself, Jean Clozel would have noticed a change in the air round him when he came out of the schoolroom during the break. Not to friendliness—an infinite distance from that—but to indifference, a stage on the way to forgetting that he had ever been a scandal and a proper treat to young creatures who had, after all, few amusements and were going to spend the rest of their lives, in a bare country, working to eat. It did not give them much time to be generous, or even amiable.

He noticed nothing. At the end of the day, when he was leaving, Marthe ran up to him, and said,

"I can't come to Black Spring this afternoon. My father has somebody he has to see in his office, and I have to stay at home to open the door to the doctor when he comes. He may not come before six. So it's no use."

"It doesn't matter," the boy said, "in fact it's just as well. I may not go myself. Or I'll go alone. I like being alone there."

She was used to him, but he was usually not so anxious to

let her know that nothing she or anyone else did or failed to do made any difference to him.

"Didn't you want me to come?" she asked naïvely. Her fine eyes held a gleam of reproach.

"I don't mind."

"Well—" she swallowed her discomfiture—"I really meant to come today. I'm sorry."

He held his hand out. "Good-by."

Astonished and laughing, she shook hands. "Why good-by? I shall see you in the morning, it's not Sunday tomorrow."

He smiled very briefly, the deliberately sarcastic smile she disliked, and walked off.

When Dr. Bertin came it was not quite five o'clock. Running to the mairie, she warned her father and went sedately back with him to the house—and the moment he shut himself in the sitting room with the doctor, to discuss, she supposed, her aunt's colic, she left again without making a sound, by the back door, to go to Black Spring.

For no reason at all, she wanted to get there as quickly as possible, and on a sudden impulse decided to save time by taking the shorter difficult way. Reckless of the uncharitable glances she knew were being turned on her between half-closed shutters —Oh, let the old cows tell Aunt Agathe what they could see, she thought—she raced down the steep street, and down the face of the hill, jumping from terrace to half-effaced terrace, to the start of the path. Along this she moved as quickly as she dare. She was both sure-footed and prudent, taking no risks ("It's not Marthe who'll stop to pray when the soup's burning" —Aunt Agathe speaking), and in fact not conscious that she was in any danger. It was only much later in her life that she could stop her heart by recalling one or two things she had done, without fear, as a child.

None the less, she sighed with relief when she was able to hurry the last few yards across the side of the hill without a precipice at her feet. She saw the boy standing at the very edge of the stream, his back to her. Running toward him, she called. He turned his head, but without smiling at her, and when she reached him all he said was, a little sulkily,

"You might as well go back. I'm going in a minute."

"Oh, you can stay a little," she said, smiling at him, "I can't stop long myself. If I'm not back to get supper ready, I shall be for it. My father wouldn't care, he's perfectly able to look after himself, but dear Aunt Agathe will tell me a million times in the same heartbroken voice that I'm thoughtless and a savage. Savage is her favorite word for me. Not that I care . . . Do sit down, Jean."

"Oh, all right. Just a minute."

The grass was burned dry and discolored; it scorched the hand laid on it, and the back of Marthe's bare legs. Immediately in front of them, a ferociously blue dragonfly clung quivering to the reeds at the edge: the feverish scraping sound coming from the buried stems was made by a pair of the lean black water rats darting in and out; for less than an instant you saw their thin snouts and one vicious eye. The river was fairly low compared with its torrential March and April, but the central current ran as alarmingly fast as ever, its surface ringed and bubbling where it passed over an unseen point of rock.

Now that she was here, there seemed less reason than ever why she had been in such a desperate hurry. It was to startle him that she said,

"I came the short way."

He frowned. "Why?"

"I don't know. I thought I would."

"You're crazy," he said.

"Have you ever done it?"

"Twice. Once is too often."

She laughed. "I shan't do it again. I don't see any point really in killing myself . . . Tell me what happened yesterday."

The glance he gave her through his eyelashes was one of pure annoyance. "Yesterday? What . . . ?"

"Your cheek."

He touched it. "You mean these marks? I fell."

"Oh, Jean, don't be a nit, and don't treat me as if I were Aunt Agathe. Do you think I don't know all about it? Clara Larrau told me what her brother told her, and—"

"Oh, very well," he interrupted coldly, "since you know everything, why ask? A few of them knocked me about, and tore my jacket. They enjoyed themselves. It's not important."

Marthe's short strong fingers curled over like claws. "I shall tell Clara to tell her clot of a brother that if he does anything like it again I'll tear his eyes out—like this."

"Well, don't do it," he said, "and don't say a word to that ferrety Larrau girl. Or I shan't tell you anything again."

But her fury had put him for a moment in a good humor, and he was laughing.

"You didn't tell me. I knew. . . . They're clots, every one of them, though—" the glance she gave him was sharp as well as caressing—"I suppose you provoked them. I heard my father talking about it to Aunt Agathe yesterday evening: they'll get used to you, he told her, it's a sort of game they play, safe for them and only dangerous for you because you are—I remembered the word to tell you—uncompromising. He means that you—"

"I know what he means, thank you," the boy said, impatiently. "I tell you it's not important, something worse, much worse, happened afterwards . . ."

He broke off, pressing his lips into a line. She waited.

"Well, what?" she asked finally.

"Nothing."

"Why won't you tell me?"

He turned toward her, without seeing her, a derisive smile. That the look of offense on his face, at the moment pale and strained, was not meant for her, she knew. She knew as much about human beings as a well-tempered child learns, living, in an isolated place, between two oversensitive disillusioned adults.

He's in one of his moods, she said to herself.

"Because."

"Oh, very well . . . But you could be polite."

"I'm sorry," he said, looking directly at her, with a sweet smile. "I'm really sorry—you're not the savage, whatever your moldy Aunt Agathe says. I am—and it's a mug's game really."

"You're stubborn."

"I can't help that, can I?"

"No, I don't suppose you can," she said lightly. "My father said you have a double dose of stubbornness in you, from both your parents. Your mother's pretty stubborn, you know, must be, or she wouldn't have fetched you here when you didn't a bit want to come."

"You call that being stubborn?"

"What do you call it?"

He did not answer. He preferred not to think of her. And in fact, since the evening before, he had not been thinking, in any deliberate way, at all; he had gone through the motions of dressing, eating, answering in class, with a sense, new to him, that he was only an onlooker at the antics of this Jean or Joachim who seemed to know where he was going and what he had to do. Good for him, the two-headed ass, since there was nothing at all in front of him.

"Let's not talk about it now." He yawned suddenly, without meaning to. "I must go."

Marthe jumped up. "Me, too. I oughtn't to be here at all."

"You can go first. I'll wait five minutes."

"Sure that's all right?"

"Yes, yes."

They walked side by side to the foot of the gorge. She left him then and began scrambling upward: glancing over her shoulder she saw him beginning to walk back toward the river.

She went on, pulling herself up by the shrubs, as rapidly as possible. He was no longer in sight. As abruptly as if she had been tapped on the shoulder she stood still, then without giving a thought to the impulse, turned and began to clamber down. The worn soles of her espadrilles sliding on the dry earth, she got to the bottom in time to see Jean, leaning far out over the river, fall into it.

He did it on purpose, she thought.

Wasting no time in shouting, she hurled herself across the short distance to the edge and jumped in.

The boy saw her do it. He struck back toward her, and caught at her dress as she came up from her plunge; the current tugged at him and he fought frenziedly to get away from it, holding her by an arm: she was going under again, and he realized briefly, too briefly to be horrified, that her thin solid little body was no better off in this stream than a twig. The noise of a rattling chain in his ears was the torrent. Gripping her hair, he made an effort that seemed to tear his lungs and heart open, felt his body lighten a little, and saw the edge of the flat rock —less than a couple of yards away. "Kick out now," he said. He felt her body move in the water, and then the rock under his hand. They clung to it together, stretching their arms across its hard smooth warmth.

"Pull yourself up."

She tried, and couldn't; he got on to it himself, dragged her up to him and rolled with her on to the grass.

They lay for minutes in each other's arms, breathing together like two exhausted little animals. Lying there, he felt rather than heard, above the sound of the river, the rippling warmth given off by the noise made by cicadas in the dry grass. At last he moved. Her arms tightened round him at once.

"No, no," he said, "it's all right, I shan't do it again."

"Swear?"

"Yes." He freed himself and sat up. "You know what? You're a rotten swimmer."

"I can't swim an inch," she said placidly, "I never learned."

"You . . ." —he glared at her. "Then why did you do that? You couldn't possibly have got me out."

Narrowing her eyes in an ingenuous smile, she said,
"Well, no, but you had to save me, didn't you?"

"Is that what you thought?"

"I didn't think."

"Marthe—"

But he had nothing to say. If he opened his mouth, the sound
that came out would be no better than a howl. He knew he
ought to thank her for her idiocy, and he knew—already—that
an abyss separated what he felt and what he would be able to
say. He sat still and let the pain hardening his throat disappear.
What it left behind it was nothing to shout about, a sort of con-
tentment, a relaxing of his body to its last nerve, and the confused notion that he could sit here, peaceably, for as long as he
lived.

"I suppose we must go," he muttered. "You'll get your death of
cold."

"In this heat?" She spread the skirt of her cotton dress round
her. "Look, I'm drying off already. But you're soaking, Jean.
What shall we do?"

He took his jacket off and wrung it, and he would have taken
off socks and shoes if he had not disliked furiously the thought
of letting her see his disfigured feet.

"Oh, it doesn't matter, I shall dry a bit on the way back. And
I can iron my suit or something, or—" he hesitated very briefly
—"she'll do it, she's very good with clothes."

"Your mother?"

"Yes."

Marthe said nothing. It occurred to her that for some little
time now he had not said: Madame Clozel. She thought vaguely:
Well, that's a mercy, he's feeling better about things. "I must
look a sight," she said, smiling.

He looked at her. Her hair was still sending trickles of water
down her neck and her round forehead, her eyes under their
thick eyebrows were very bright and her cheeks crimson. She
smelled of mud and wild mint.

"You look like a gypsy."

She laughed out. "I think you mean a savage."

"No."

"I'm as hungry as a savage, aren't you? Let's go."

They climbed together up the goat path to the road. Neither of them so much as glanced at the monument with its bunch of flowers: fresh that morning, when an old woman laid them down, they were already dead of the heat. It was on principle that Jean Clozel avoided looking at it, putting off the day when he would be forced to ask someone, probably Marthe herself, to tell him about it. To Marthe it meant as much and as little as the list nailed up in the church, names of the dead of two wars, 1870-71, and 1914-18, both equally far off.

When they had been walking for a few minutes, the boy said, "If we arrive together in this state, and somebody sees us, they'll never stop asking questions. Do you mind?"

"Not a mite."

"All the same," he said, frowning, "you'd better go on ahead."

"If you like."

His frown became a scowl pulling his eyebrows into a single black line. "Marthe. If it had been like it was in March we shouldn't have had a hope. I should have drowned us both. I very nearly did as it was, and I promise I shan't forget it, what you did, and that by now I'd be stone dead. . . . I'll explain it to you one of these days, but I can't now."

"Well, neither of us is drowned," she said calmly.

They looked at each other for a moment with simulated unconcern, then Marthe said, smiling,

"All right, I'll run on now. See you tomorrow."

"See you tomorrow."

He watched her hurry, half running, along the dusty rough road, then turned to look back. It must be seven and after, he thought. The air was cooler, and a superb trick of the declining light had brought the mountains to look over the shoulders of less distant lower hills, a line of sharply pointed crests, the highest gleaming with snow; everything below them was a mosaic of shifting greens, blues, mauves, with delicate bronze and black veins, like an exotic marble. A dry scent of resin and crushed thyme came from the harsh bare country behind the cindery pasture belonging to old Larrau. As hard as the hardest thing in the world, this country, he thought, but it's not bad: she might have been thinking of it when she talked about the force of things. Probably not, though. What *does* she think about when she's alone? . . . About me, he thought, frowning; about that camp they sent her to after I . . . Oh, yes, she's stubborn, she must have needed it to put up with me.

He had a moment of complete lucidity, during which he thought: I can bear it, I can bear anything.

He turned back. Marthe was out of sight, and he followed slowly, the discomfort of damp clothes and sodden shoes floating in his mind on the surface of a deep indifference to anything except the fact that he was alive and able to feel. The warm light breeze that started up here in the evening now excited him a little, stroking the back of his neck as he walked, head bent, hurrying.

When he opened the door into her room she was there, knitting: she glanced at him and glanced away—in this dark room, its one small window looking out on to the narrow street, she did not notice the state of his clothes—and said,

"Your jacket's in your room—if you want to look at it before supper. It's all right."

Expecting that he would go upstairs at once, she kept her head down. An obscure feeling of warmth kept him standing there: for the first time he was discovering that to be in a position to comfort somebody you have hurt is acutely pleasant, a sensual pleasure.

"What are you making?" he asked.

She looked up quickly. "A sweater."

"For me?"

"Yes. It gets terribly cold here in winter."

He stooped and fingered it. "It's nice," he said, smiling. "I shall like it."

The crazy joy that came into her face, its faded skin suddenly flushed, embarrassed him. He touched her hand briefly, and went away. In his own room, he stood for a moment thinking in a confused way that he was going to live here a long time, years, and everything, himself included, would have changed before he was able to go away. Instinctively, he spread his long thin hands, as if to let the days slip one at a time between his fingers, instead of crushing him with their whole weight. As for this afternoon—Never again, he said to himself, never never again.

He took his time about changing his clothes, and when he was ready to go downstairs—he could hear her moving about the kitchen, between stove and table—he hesitated an instant, his hand on the knob of the door, and said under his breath,

"Don't be afraid, I shall always, whatever changes, love you better than anyone. But if you could see her now, you would be sorry for her, too."

Then he opened the door quickly and went down.

20

On the November evening when Aristide Michal went to say good-by to the Englishman, a drying south wind had thrown the advancing winter back into the Alps: it was still autumn, the iron-veined autumn of this Provençal hill country, a little warmth in the soil under the grass and tall brittle herbs, the few trees more green than bronze, with here and there a group of cypresses still supple, still flowing like plumes. In the gray darkness before moonrise, the car lamps lit up only what might have been the edge of an African desert.

He had not set eyes on Leighton for more than a month—the Englishman had ceased to dine at the hotel, sending by Ahmed a message that he was too old, neither his throat nor his stomach had any longer the courage to enjoy good food—and during this month he had changed a great deal, a change going, Michal thought, to the skeleton. Not that, to go so far, it had had to make more than one bound. In the five deep hollows of his head, at the temples, at the back of the neck, and below the cheek-bones, the flesh, what there was of it, had taken on the color of clay, and his great beak of a nose now shared his face with the high forehead topped by its thick gray comb; nothing else, not even his eyes, was noticeable, except when now and then a flash from those pale eyes called to mind a claw moving at the back of a rock crevice.

Now what we are seeing is the man himself, Michal thought. Not that he ever, at any time, told himself or us lies, but now he is reduced to his essence. He is someone of very great quality, an aristocrat.

Setting down carefully the bottles of good claret, four of his last six, he said,

"I know you don't like gifts, Monsieur Leighton, but this time you are making me a gift by accepting. I have kept two back, and I propose to drink them tomorrow night, before I go."

"Thank you," Leighton said. "If you think we can open one at once, it will make the meal you are about to eat a great deal more palatable. Ahmed has two dishes, a kind of omelette and a mess of rice and fish. I believe you are getting the second."

"There are at least two women in the village who could cook for you."

Leighton smiled sardonically. "How long do you imagine Ahmed would tolerate one of them in his kitchen? There would be a mysterious accident, she'd be found one evening, her neck and all her bones broken, at the bottom of the quarry across the road. . . . I don't eat more than a few mouthfuls, and I prefer soup, so that I'm indifferent."

"All the same, I was sorry you didn't taste my last dinner," Michal said, smiling. "It was masterly—ask Monsieur Gaudo."

"I believe you. . . . What are your plans?"

"For the moment—none. After a month or two, I can choose—" His smile became naïvely frank and arrogant. "A chef of my quality doesn't go begging."

"I suppose not," Leighton said a little dryly. "You'll stay in this neighborhood?"

"No."

"Why not?"

"You don't need to ask. For more than one reason. And because I don't care to start again where I'm known—where what has happened is known."

Leighton gave him a cruelly speculative glance. His affection for the other man could not blunt the edge of his cold mind. "Yes. It must be a bitter pill to give up a place where you've been triumphantly successful."

"It was very bitter," Michal said calmly, "and I've swallowed it. What's more, having got it down, I feel unconcerned, even happy. The only thing I should find insufferable would be starting again as a subordinate, forced to take orders. That risk apart, I'm perfectly happy."

There was no doubting his sincerity. Leighton felt a mixture of respect and amusement. He did not believe in the possibility of a happiness lying at the other, the farther side of despair and bitterness, and he was surprised that a man as shrewd as the Greek could deceive himself. It is his vanity, he thought: even a man as solid, aggressive, adroit, cannot look himself in the face for long. He kept back a smile.

"I read yesterday's account of the trial," he said. "And I hear that today it was all over by four o'clock, and your wife acquitted of—" he hesitated—"any connection with the robbery. I'm immensely relieved."

"Ah, you've been told?"

"Monsieur Pibourdin gave himself the pleasure of calling on me an hour ago. He was in court throughout the trial—both days."

"Trust him!"

(Too delighted by having got his foot inside this house where he had never been a guest to notice that Leighton was eying him with distaste, Pibourdin laid himself out to be amusing. "When I was listening to Maître Rodier's moving recital of the virtues and motherly soul of Madame Michal I was almost prepared myself to swear that she was a warmhearted child of nature led astray, not too far astray, by her tenderness for others. For the whole world!")

"She was certainly connected with it," Michal said slowly, "in so far as she held her tongue—but it would have been unjust to punish her."

"If the case had been heard in England she would have been punished—mildly, no doubt, but punished. In some ways—when it is taking human nature into account—French procedure is infinitely more humane than ours. More human, let's say."

Michal was silent. When he brought her home, Lotte was able to walk swiftly from the car to their room—pausing in the shut-up café to speak with smiling coldness to Thérèse and Madame Truchi, who were exalted far beyond discretion and stuttered on about the mercy of God and the goodness of St. Anthony—but as soon as she was inside the room, and the door shut, she collapsed as if she had had a stroke, falling forward on the bed. It was not the kind of collapse, like a beaten animal, or the kind of agony, she went through when she was exposing herself in front of Philippe; this was the despair and grief, bottomless, of a child who has lost something by its own fault, has no one but itself to blame, and can do nothing to help itself. Her face, without powder, without rouge on its long mouth, was that of an aging clown. At one moment, when she caught sight of herself in the glass, she began crying and could not stop. "I'm old, I'm old," she said in a small hoarse voice. "Look at the old fool, who'd have thought I could cry like this for a . . . for a . . ."

Michal tried reasoning with her. "Who are you crying for? For the boy? For yourself?"

"For all of us—for the mess I've made of things, the idiocy, the spoiling of your life—and mine."

"Rubbish," he said gently, "my life isn't spoiled. Altered, if you like, but not spoiled."

"Oh, no, no," she stammered, "I wish I was dead."

"Oh, no, you don't, you don't in the least want to be dead.

That's only words. You'll find tomorrow that what you want is something a good deal harder and of more use."

He might have been talking to a stone. She was, as the two old women would have said, past herself, all the fears, shames, humiliation, strain, of the past months pushing her to an extremity of self-loathing. It occurred to him that, in this state, he could probably get anything out of her—the truth—so far as there is one truth about any act of a human being: did she plot with Philippe to ruin him, or was she truly a dupe, truly startled and reluctant when he brought the other two into her room that night, perhaps, he thought with an instant's savage resentment, when she expected to see him coming in alone?

With the question on the end of his tongue he kept his mouth shut. Not that he felt a compunction about making use of her state to question her. Brutal it might be, but he could justify it to himself. He had a right to the truth. But . . .

Do I want the truth? he asked himself. If I knew, knew, that she was a deliberate accomplice, could I go on living with her? And is there any point in punishing her further for her weakness, for the trap it led her into?

He felt a revulsion which had nothing to do with any pity for her, or any tenderness. What it comes down to, he thought, is —I daren't ask.

He gave up trying to soothe her by talking. Instead, he went down to the kitchen, made coffee, buttered a slice of bread, and brought them upstairs to her. When he came in with them, she sat up, arching her back, and tried to drink the coffee, but her hand shook so uncontrollably that she put the cup down. Going on one knee, Michal spooned the coffee between her dry lips as if helping a child to drink, and held the bread for her to swallow mouthfuls of it. After this, he undressed her and put her to bed, pulling the quilt round her. In her dazed exhaustion, she made no attempt to help him, beyond holding her arms out for him to pull her chemise over her head. She fell asleep almost at once, a heap of tired humbled flesh. Drawing his hand from hers, he left her there, and went down to the cellar to get the claret he meant to give Leighton. . . .

He became aware of Leighton as a predatory beak and cruelly bright eyes.

"I shall never know," he said, "whether she helped to plot the robbery or was drawn into it."

Beyond a nod, Leighton made no answer to this brief, bitterly ironic confidence. He asked coolly,

"Are you taking her with you?"

"Yes, of course. One of the reasons for not staying in the neighborhood. Now that so many people know everything, or almost everything, about her, she would find it"—he laughed shortly—"less pleasant."

"Y'know," Leighton said carelessly, "your people—I mean the old Greeks—knew, or suspected, that women have a closer relation with the more irrational gods than we have. Split the atom, land on the moon, but women will always be exactly what they were in Homer's time. It makes no difference how one treats them, loyally, kindly, disloyally, neglectfully, they remain hopelessly amoral and anarchic and private. This has its good side, of course—they're not so easily taken in by idealists. But I wonder who or what possesses them, what unscrupulous or joking god or goddess. I take it that they have more nature than we have. If you outrage or bore nature, it hits back. Goodness or badness doesn't enter into it—objectively, what they do may be good or bad; they themselves are neither."

"So, if they ruin our lives, we should look to see who is grinning behind them," Michal said.

He put his head back and roared with laughter. No need, thought Leighton, to pity him; he doesn't need it, he's all action himself, action and self-possession and energy and a touch of the buffoon.

He waited until Ahmed, moving behind their chairs as quietly as if he were one of the shadows of the ill-lit room, had taken away the mess of rice—his portion of it barely tasted—and was setting out cheese and a dish of dried figs. Then he said gently,

"I haven't spoken about the boy. They were bound to give him a fairly stiff sentence—partly because of that old woman and her money. Can't have dollar-carrying visitors being robbed. There was nothing you could do for him."

"Nothing," Michal said. He added in a ferociously restrained and hard voice, "I failed with him. No use going overboard. I propose to see him when he comes out, and if there's anything I can do I'll do it. If not . . ."

He made a gesture with his hands as if balancing a weight. He still cares more for that boy than for the woman, Leighton thought: if he had to lose one of them he'd infinitely sooner it had been her. He'll survive, though. . . . He looked hard at Michal, trying to see details he would forget as one forgets the details of a painting: the darkly tanned skin, the long splendidly curling moustache giving him the look of a Greek sea captain, the big supple body, the eyes in which gaiety or anger set off a spurt of yellow flame. There is more to him than I knew, he thought. Until now, he had barely appreciated an inborn delicacy and subtlety underlying the other's shrewdness, his egoism and vanity, his resilience, his lighthearted skepticism.

He is a most generous man, he said to himself. I didn't realize it.

"God damn it," he said abruptly, "life is an absurd business. We spend the whole of it scheming and struggling, and die in the end like an animal. No, no, it's inacceptable. . . . As a boy I was taught that human nature is mellowing, we can pat ourselves on the back, friends. The proof—we no longer burn heretics. Then comes Belsen, and the herds of gassed and tortured men and women and children finished off like dogs. And Hiroshima. And future Hiroshimas. So much for progress! I tell you—but you know it—the great causes, the dignity of man, defense of freedom and the rest and the rest, lead straight to the dung heap."

Michal twisted an end of his great mustache round a long hard finger. "Perhaps," he said carelessly.

"Perhaps!" Leighton pulled an insultingly derisive face. "The joke of it is that when a country refuses to defend its freedom some less civilized nation comes along and cuts its throat. Disgust at the thought of killing is something tolerant old men feel, they die or are killed off, and the young and savage take over —and off we go again. Tolerance makes you tolerate those who will crucify you. The end is always bloody. Always."

"So what?" Michal said, smiling.

"Nothing. Nothing, nothing."

"You're very sure of your nothing," Michal said. He smiled again and drank. "I don't know why you should be—since we shall never know the truth. My advice is: Leave it alone, and leave other people alone, so far as you can. Things are as they are. And some of them are always worth having—a good dinner, a fine day, a woman when you can't do without one, a glass of water. No, no, I've no complaints."

"How old are you?" Leighton mocked. "Wait until you're my age."

Wait, he thought, until your animal fierceness and energy are down to their last layer of ash. He felt a prick of anger.

"Don't think I keep my eyes shut!" Michal exclaimed. "If I were being shoved by a healthy young brute into a gas chamber I shouldn't say to myself that so far things hadn't been too bad. Yet in my case it would be true! I've had a good life. You know what the old women say: Ten sorrows to every happiness. And man is a handful of grass and so on and so on and so what. It's a short life and ends badly—all right, all right—but on the way there what a show, eh, what a show!"

"You're a hardened egoist, my friend."

"Because I'm happy?" Michal said, grinning.

He had drunk the greater share of the bottle, and Leighton made a sign to Ahmed to open another.

"On the whole, yes. Happiness like yours is egoism."

Michal frowned in his effort to be honest without offense. "It's true I don't kick against the facts—but neither do I go on my knees and say: Thy will be done. I'm as capable as the next man of behaving like a brute. And capable of checking myself —and of cutting his throat to check him. What more can I do? There's a law of life—"

Cocking his head on one side like a good-humored vulture, Leighton said,

"And what do *you* know about the law of life?"

"Nothing at all! But you can't tell me there isn't one. In the end those who go too far get what's coming to them. I say: in the end."

"You may be right. Heaven forbid I should say a word to corrupt your naïveté—I'm a cynic, but I detest cynicism. Go on being happy!"

Michal laughed gently. "You're not drinking," he said. "Don't you like this claret?"

"It's excellent. Lately I've had a little difficulty in swallowing." He touched his throat.

It crossed Michal's mind that this was an old difficulty. Had the other man ever been (as they say) alive and present? Ever been on friendly terms with his senses, the whole range, from the acts of sex to the taste of decent bread? Hadn't he—between them and him, between him and his own life—hadn't he willfully let in disenchantment, suspicion, self-dislike? Now he was refusing to live at all, except in a past he couldn't swallow.

He could not put into words his rush of affection for this old surely dying man, and his wish to comfort him. If he tried, the Englishman would only jeer at him.

"What d'you think of me?" Leighton asked abruptly.

"Perhaps you're too intelligent. You haven't the solid layer of flesh that keeps me sane."

"Nonsense. We're both ruined, we've both made fools of ourselves. What's to be done about it, eh?"

Barely touching them with the ends of his narrow fingers,

Ahmed moved plates and refilled the glasses and went away. Leighton closed his eyes. At once, his face became tranquil, almost appealing, as though he had closed them in the expectation of a caress.

Michal kept quiet. For no reason—unless this evening were their first chance to dodge past a lifetime of ceaseless hard work —a few images from his farthest past started up. He saw a cluster of houses hanging over a ravine, not unlike St.-Loup-de-Grâce, the same faded browns, ivory, rose, the same tiled roofs, the same corroded hillside, heat, olives, a few, a very few vines. But the people here are not like Greece, he thought, or rather felt: they're softer, crueler, greedier. . . . Then for less than a moment he saw the cracked shutters of the house he lived in with grand-parents and an uncle, two rooms, one above the other like Madeleine Clozel's house, but shabbier and poorer, an earthen floor downstairs and discolored white walls; below it, falling down the side of the ravine, a fleece of sun-bleached roofs: in the same instant he saw his grandfather's face, an old dark wrinkled parchment, with a mustache like the horns of a ram. His uncle's face of that time eluded him, blotted out by an excess of light. It came back to him suddenly: he was cradled in a very young man's arm, and the young man was seated side-ways on a donkey, facing not the steep road but a stone wall; a yellow flower grew from a cranny and he cried to be given it, looking up into the laughing face bent over him . . .

As swiftly as it had risen up out of time the image vanished, swept past like a fleck of foam. Did I get the flower? he wondered. A sense of warmth and safety filled him.

He had an obscure sense of two streams flowing underground, one of them starting at the other side of Europe in the, to him, unimaginable childhood of the old Englishman, to meet at this moment in a shadowy underworld. Like an underworld bat, Leighton's despair brushed him. He has missed the goodness of life, he thought: Langadhia, the laughing boy, the sun, the intensely clear light, the old voices . . .

Leaning across the table, he touched Leighton's hand briefly. It was not easy to do, he had too much respect for the Englishman, but the other man was so alone.

"Enjoy yourself, my old friend," he said.

"It's too late."

"Not until the last minute!"

"I must tell you something," Leighton said in a low voice. "You remember the book I told you I'd finished. Well, I've destroyed it."

Groping for inoffensive words, Michal said, "That was extremely generous."

"Bosh," Leighton said rudely and coldly. "I did it only to please myself. And I don't even know that I did the right or the sensible thing. The fact is," he went on in a brutally mocking voice, "our virtues, or what we think are our virtues, ruin us as quickly as our supposed vices. If you hadn't picked up an abandoned child, if you hadn't trusted your woman, if I hadn't befriended a little tart . . . excess is always punished, eh? Your famous law of life. Including excessive pity . . . No one ruins our lives, we do it too easily ourselves. My late dear wife didn't ruin me, my pity for her did it. I should have kicked her out, told her and her ambassador to pay their own entrance fee, slept with another woman at once and bred children . . ."

"If we had done this, if we hadn't done that," said Michal violently. "All absurd. We couldn't in decency have done anything else."

"Decency is beside the point," Leighton said.

"Not more than regrets. We do what our bodies tell us— neither of us could have acted differently. In the end—"

He hesitated, and Leighton said harshly,

"In the end?"

"Oh—in the end you play the cards put into your hand, and leave it at that."

A silence. I should go, Michal thought. He stood up.

"When are you leaving the village?" Leighton asked.

"The day after tomorrow."

"Come in for a glass of your own wine before you go, you and Madame Michal."

"We're leaving much too early. I don't want spectators."

"I'm awake at three," Leighton said. He smiled.

Dead, he'll smile no differently, Michal thought. He reflected that he had seen faces of the dead which seemed only to be closing their eyes against the light. Leighton's would not be like that.

"Very well," he said, "I'll look in."

He stepped out of the half-dark house into moonlight, an unusually splendid light, he thought, the sky cloudless and high, flowing away overhead to an horizon closed by what seemed curves of mist with one dark acropolis breaking through. The shadows, thrown across the road, of a mountain ash still in leaf and a tall shrub, had several depths of blackness, one below the other. He drove without switching on the lights. At one moment a hare crossed the blindingly white road, its ears and strong forelegs etched in the finest of fine dark lines on the light, and a moth, a tiny transparent moth, brushed the windscreen and fled away unharmed. There was even a current of warmth in the air.

Why, he asked himself, should I suppose that I shan't see him again?

The empty café and the bedroom were filled by the same fleecy light. Lotte was sound asleep. When he closed the shutters and turned the lamp on, she moved, sighed, and fell back into sleep. Looking down at her, he thought: She'll be all serene in the morning. Nothing like a sound sleep.

21

No one in the village—except Leighton—knew that this was their last evening; they intended to get away without giving anyone the pleasure of going through the motions of attending a funeral. Never had Michal felt less like the role of victim. Nor had he any need to play the part of a man freed from burdens; he really did feel liberated and his gaiety hid only a few grains of regret.

"What do you want for supper?" he asked Lotte.

"An omelette," she said carelessly, "some red wine."

"Good."

They ate in the kitchen, at the long scrubbed table, scored across and across by the edge of knives so sharp that they broke the skin of the wood at a touch. Filling her glass, he said,

"There are two bottles of claret and one of the 1911 armagnac to be drunk this evening. Good management." He looked round the room, smiling a little. "It's been very pleasant here for seventeen years, eh?"

"Yes," Lotte said, "we had a good life." The ironic lines at the ends of her mouth deepened. "Too good."

He laughed. "So it was time for the balance to tip, eh?"

"Not for you. What did *you* do wrong?"

"Who knows?" he said, drinking.

"It's unjust—there was no reason to punish you."

"You're a fool," he said with ironic gentleness—the irony for himself, the gentleness less for her than for a familiar object he used for living, "no one is being punished. Go on drinking. We're not quite penniless, we have enough for two or three months, and no obligations, we can go anywhere we like. In fact, this isn't the end of things, it's the beginning."

"*You* can say so," she murmured, "you didn't fall so far as I did."

The actual process of losing your illusions about yourself— that you're a fine fellow, too shrewd to be cheated, with an admiring wife—is painful, even agonizing, but their loss is in a sense a release. Not, I suppose, for a woman, he thought: without her illusions about herself she feels unattractive and lost.

"My dear girl," he said gaily, "think of your luck, you're as free as air, your blunders and worst needs are behind you, all you have to do for the rest of your life is look, taste, touch, smell —and you have all your organs intact." He touched her cheek. "And there are two of us."

"Yes," she said, with a brief laugh. "But wouldn't you rather be without me?"

"No."

"Why not?"

He shrugged his shoulders. "Don't ask too many questions. Give me your glass."

She pushed it toward him. "I must ask," she said quietly. "*Why* didn't you kick me out? You'd be better off without me, you could marry a young woman, have children—a different life."

"Maybe so, but . . ." He looked at her in friendly derision. "What is this nonsense? Do you want to be turned off?"

"No."

"Very well, then."

"I'm afraid of loneliness," she said in a light oddly impersonal voice. "When you come to think, that's three quarters of our lives. That, and the not being sure of anyone."

"I know it—" he was laughing—"and two bodies are better than one. At least you can be sure of that."

If of nothing else, he thought. And even if bodily warmth, companionship and the rest are only a mask over the isolation and cold. But what's wrong with that?

"After all," she said, "you knew me when I was a young woman."

"After all?"

"Before all. A woman of my age—who else would want me?"

"So you feel grateful, eh?"

"No," Lotte said.

She had said it in the voice, deep, powerful, rough, precise, which could still move him a little.

"Good," he said dryly.

Suppose, he thought, drinking, there really is nothing—at our age—except habit and loneliness, the important thing is not to admit it. What a figure I cut, he thought easily, the cuckold, the ass cheated out of his money, and how little I care . . . In an obscure way, he shared her knowledge of her aging body, her shame. There was nothing he could do; the woman he had known for years and for some years violently loved, had disappeared—except for her voice, for the light smell of cedar. Forget her, he thought, forget her and be a little sorry . . . But nothing irritated him more than to be suspected, or to suspect himself, of pitying her. As ridiculous as it was—as he was—he preferred to cherish her. Not for anything she could give him —what more could she give him than any personable woman he might put his hand on? For what he could give her. My company in bed and at table, he thought, grinning; I still have a body and the rest of it, and a tongue in my head.

"Ah," he said, with a sort of rage, "trust yourself, trust me

—we're going to wear ourselves out, to the last shred of energy, and enjoy it. D'you believe me?"

To his surprised delight she broke into her deep throaty laugh, a sound he had not heard for a long time. "Yes, yes."

"Don't you want to know where we're going?" he asked her.

"You said—Marseilles."

"You didn't think we were going to stop there? We can go anywhere, every road's open—but we'll start with Greece. What d'you say? We might even stay there." He laughed. "Show them how to cook."

They had reached the armagnac. "If I drink any more," Lotte said, "I shall be drinking far too much."

"Nonsense."

"It's true." She stood up. "Finish it yourself, I'm going to bed."

"Very well. When it's finished I'll come."

He watched her go. When all the ordinary reasons for living were on their way out, when he could no longer enjoy sleeping with her, stretching himself in the sun, drinking, there would remain, he was sure of it, a single strand between them, arbitrary, a little ridiculous, as he was himself, but, this side of the final gesture, indestructible.

They left the house—no longer the Hotel Moderne Aristide, but a strong shabby house awaiting its "foreigner"—soon after five o'clock. A colorless light filled the village street, coming from uneven layers of clear cold sky. Michal's body, after its short sleep, was alert and cool. He remembered his promise to the Englishman and instead of turning left out of the square, to go toward Grasse, he turned right. The narrow stony track climbing to Leighton's house was off the road, a mile beyond the village, opposite the disused quarry: trees masked the low-built house itself and the first thing they saw when he swung the car round them was Dr. Bertin's old black Peugeot, in front of the door, which had been left standing open.

Michal stopped the car, but did not get out. He waited, without surprise, calmly. Ahmed came to the door. He stood there for a second and lifted his arms, the long thin dark hands turned upward, then let them drop to his side, the gesture of a woman.

"Are you going in?" Lotte asked.

"No." He began turning the car. "No, we'll go on."

ABOUT THE AUTHOR

Storm Jameson (Margaret Storm Jameson) was born in Whitby, Yorkshire, England. After taking honors in English at Leeds University she was awarded a research scholarship to work on modern European drama at King's College in London. For a time she was a copy writer, wrote dramatic criticism, was a publisher, then became a full-time novelist. She is married to Guy Patterson Chapman, formerly Professor of Modern History at Leeds University.